LAW AND ARDOR

THE BEELER LARGE PRINT MYSTERY SERIES

Edited by Audrey A. Lesko

9/04

DATE DUE

2/19/05			
7-5-05			
NOV 0 6 2006			
3-22			
12/10/08			
11-21-13			

DEMCO 13829810

LAW AND ARDOR

An Andrew Broom Mystery

Ralph McInerny

BEELER LARGE PRINT

Hampton Falls, New Hampshire, 2001

Library of Congress Cataloging-in-Publication Data

McInerny, Ralph M.
  Law and ardor / Ralph McInerny.
      p.   cm.—(The Beeler Large Print mystery series)
  ISBN 1-57490-410-8 (alk. paper)
  1. Broom, Andrew (Fictitious character)—Fiction.
2. Indiana—Fiction. 3. Large type books. I. Title. II. Series.

  PS3563.A31166 L37 2001
  813'.54—dc21   2001043537

Published in Large Print by arrangement with Scribner, an imprint of Simon & Schuster Inc.

BEELER LARGE PRINT
is published by
Thomas T. Beeler, Publisher
Post Office Box 659
Hampton Falls, New Hampshire 03844

Typeset in 16 point Times New Roman type.
Printed on acid-free paper, sewn and bound by
Sheridan Books in Chelsea, Michigan.

For Helen and Jim Hitchcock

ONE

THE BODY OF EDGAR BISSONET WAS FOUND LYING ON the seventh fairway of the Wyler Country Club. The cart in which he had been riding was parked beside the body, its battery completely run down. Edgar himself, dressed with his customary panache for golf—plus fours, plaid sleeveless sweater, yellow shirt open at the neck, and black-and-white perforated golf shoes—was lying facedown with a sand wedge grasped in a hand gone stiff with rigor mortis. The body was discovered by three members who disdained electric carts and were pulling their clubs on wheeled carts, a practice frowned upon by the committee because it slowed up the game. But playing as early as they did, this could hardly be considered a factor.

"What the hell is that cart doing in the middle of the fairway?" Will Abner asked.

"What cart?" asked Jim Bullock, peering into the early morning haze.

"Just off the sand trap," Tom McCoy answered.

"Swing away then," Bullock advised. "We're not going to hit a ball that far."

So they drove, putting their balls out 125, 130, and 170 yards from the tee, not bad for men in their late seventies. Slowly, they set off from the tee, leaving wavering trails from the wheels of their carts, happy to be alive and on the course.

"What's that next to the goddam cart?" Abner asked, as he neared his ball. He was not much of a driver but he had a seven wood that performed marvels.

"I see the cart now," Bullock said.

1

"Looks like a man."

"Lying on the ground."

"Maybe he's lining up his approach and intends to hole out."

So they went cackling to their balls and sent them on their way in the general direction of the green. Abner took a sweeping swing with his trusty seven wood, caught the ball cleanly, and sent it on a wide hooking drive into the rough just short of the green.

"Great shot," his companions grudgingly called.

"I lost my footing a bit," Abner said, but he was grinning with the result of the shot.

Bullock scuffed his second and immediately asked where his ball had gone. He seemed to expect a different result than he got.

"I didn't even see it. I would have sworn I got a good hit."

McCoy, the long ball hitter of the threesome, stroked a three iron that started low and was rising beautifully when it hit the parked golf cart and careened left into the sand trap.

"I'm going to kill that sonofabitch," McCoy said and, jaw outthrust, began pulling his clubs toward the parked cart.

"Let me hit my ball," Bullock complained, and McCoy halted, but he still pointed at the offending cart as if fearful his wrath would cool.

Bullock hit a worm burner that went between the cart and the sand trap and kept on going, sending up a nice plume of dew as it scuttled through the grass.

"Fore!" Bullock called belatedly.

"He's not moving," Abner observed.

"Hey!" McCoy shouted, as he closed on his prey. But then he slowed and stopped and waited for the others to catch up. He had a premonition that something was amiss.

The three stood six feet short of the cart, staring at the body of the man who was stretched facedown on the dewy grass.

"Who is he?" Bullock asked.

McCoy said he'd have to see his face, but Abner said the outfit gave him away. That was Edgar Bissonet.

"Edgar," he called. "You all right, Edgar?"

Bullock had been retired from medicine for nearly fifteen years, having made his pile and gotten out, but he had not forgotten everything.

"He's dead, you idiot."

They inched closer and McCoy crouched beside the body.

"Don't touch him," Bullock cautioned.

McCoy, robbed of the chance of blaming the man for what had happened to his second shot, looked angrily at Bullock. "Don't worry."

"Is it Edgar?"

McCoy turned his cheek horizontally to the ground, then lowered his head carefully. Half a minute went by. "Edgar?" he said softly.

"The man's dead," Bullock said, coming closer, but careful not to touch the body. Residual memories of malpractice insurance pricked at the edges of his mind.

"His eyes are open."

"They usually are."

A conference ensued as to what they should do. Bullock, who was already fifteen over par, thought they ought to head back to the clubhouse and report the body.

"Hell, he lives right over there," Abner said, pointing to the houses that lined this fairway. "He just drives onto the course here and starts playing."

3

"Can he do that?"

"He does it. Wirth was complaining about it." Wirth was the club pro.

"You want to go over, knock on the door, and tell a woman her husband is lying dead on fairway seven?"

"No, I sure don't want to do that."

McCoy thought they ought to finish the nine. That would take them toward the clubhouse anyway, and after they putted out on nine they could sound the alarm.

"That's pretty hard-hearted."

"Hell, it'll take us just as long to walk in."

It was Abner who looked back at the seventh tee. "That twosome has caught up with us."

"It's not our fault . . ."

"Can you see if they have an electric cart?" Bullock asked.

"Sure they do."

"Let's wave them through," Bullock said, looking shrewd. "It'll be easier for them to ride into the clubhouse and we can just continue our game."

So they shuffled off to the side of the fairway, and made great sweeping arcs with their arms, signaling the twosome to come ahead. But there was no movement on the tee.

"They're bothered by that cart."

"We can't move it."

"Do they think they can reach it?"

McCoy said, "Do you know who that is? That's Andrew Broom."

That settled it. They kept signaling Andrew on and he and his partner delayed, but finally teed up and hit.

"God, what a drive," Abner said.

"I can't see it," Bullock complained. "Where'd it go?"

"It's still going."

4

It was a high powerful shot that went fifty yards beyond where they were standing and continued to roll after it landed.

"That's close to three hundred yards," McCoy said reverently.

Andrew's partner hit a clone of Andrew's drive and then the cart was headed toward them. The threesome got into the fairway again.

"What a drive," Abner said as Broom approached. "You really kissed that baby."

"What's that cart doing in the fairway?"

"It was there when we came along."

"Is that someone lying beside it?"

"Edgar Bissonet."

"What's wrong with him?"

"He's dead."

TWO

SUSANNAH REFUSED TO BELIEVE THE STORY WHEN Andrew told her later, and he could hardly blame her. It was like a bad golf joke: Hit, drag George, hit, drag George.

"Gerald is my witness."

For a man with the exaggerated dignity of Edgar Bissonet, it was a farcical way to leave this world and that particular point on it, Wyler, Indiana, where he had lived his long, calculating, and prosperous life. There was special irony in the fact that, although Andrew Broom had once been Edgar's lawyer, there had been a misunderstanding and the old man had switched to Andrew's arch rival Frank McGough. Yet it was Andrew who sent Gerald on to the clubhouse to fetch

5

help and was to wait by the body of his former client until it was duly examined and eventually carried away by Evans the undertaker and coroner.

"That is his house just over yonder," Bullock said.

"Yes, it is."

"One of us could go tell his missus what has happened."

"Would you want to do that, Bullock?"

"My God, no."

"He died in sight of his house," Abner remarked, a tone of awe in his voice.

"I suppose there's no reason the three of us couldn't just finish our game," McCoy said.

"You'd better wait until the police get here," Andrew said.

"The police? I thought you sent for an ambulance."

"Well, after all, we have a medical man in our midst. Have you examined him, Bullock?"

"I saw that he was dead."

"No pulse?"

"No need to take a pulse when rigor mortis has already set in. Look at the grip on that club."

"It's a wedge," Abner noted.

"A sand wedge," McCoy added.

The conversation with the three old men, a little jittery perhaps, having been so forcefully reminded of their own end and peeved to have their habitual morning round disturbed, was dull enough, about on a par with what is said at wakes, out of earshot of the relatives. Although they were much the same age as Edgar, none of the three seemed to have known him well. Andrew, on the other hand, for professional and personal reasons, would have said that he had known Edgar Bissonet all too well.

6

✱✱✱

The small town, like the family farm, is not what it was—there are fewer of them and those that still exist are bent on becoming as citified as possible. And, as with the farm, it is difficult to keep young people in a small town. They go off to school and their vistas widen so that at graduation their ambitions are pretty much those of their city cousins. Eventually, with prosperity, they will hope to move out of the city and into something like the town in which they were raised. As a place to raise their own children, perhaps.

Wyler was in this respect atypical. It held its population and it held its traditions. In the country at large, racial differences apart, there are few social distinctions left, save those of money. The income one makes establishes one's place in society, and one can move up and down the scale with ease as money is gained or lost. The moneyed move into newly created housing developments where the garish houses and large lots serve as indexes of wealth. Less money, less house, different neighborhood, until the scale drops down into urban blight. For those who remain in the city, the pecking order is established by the size, location, and price of one's apartment. But here, too, mobility is the rule, and the suddenly successful live cheek by jowl with old money—money made as long ago as ten years, perhaps.

In the small town, the class system still obtains to some degree. One is born into a certain level of society, and not many move upward or downward in their lifetimes. Sudden wealth, such as Oscar Beiger, for instance, had acquired with the purchase of four fast-food-franchises, did not alter Oscar's position in Wyler society. If he were to apply for membership in the

7

country club, a way would be found to refuse him. But of course since Oscar would know this, he would save himself and the members the trouble and not apply at all.

Edgar Bissonet was not Oscar Beiger, but he was decidedly from the Wyler lower middle class. His prosperity had brought him to a lovely house along the seventh fairway but it was the fact that he had married Jane Spencer that explained his membership in the club. The Spencers had not been unreservedly happy with the match, a fact that may very well have contributed to the ambition that had marked Edgar's life.

He had begun in the trust department at the Wyler First National and gone on to start his own brokerage. Once Andrew had a small account with him and it had done well—well enough that he had thought of putting a good deal more with Edgar—but since Edgar was then a client, Andrew decided against it. Now Edgar's son Matthew was in effective charge of Bissonet Brokers, leaving Edgar time for the leisure he had never allowed himself. Once he decided to have fun, Edgar put his heart and soul into it, and the principal path of dalliance he had chosen was golf. He indulged in the latest equipment, the allegedly most fashionable toggery, and endless lessons from poor Wirth.

"Is he improving?" Andrew had asked Wirth.

"You have to do a thing first before you can get better at it," Wirth had responded.

Gerald Rowan, Andrew's nephew, whom he had induced to come to Wyler and join his firm, was mystified by the intricate social structure of the small town.

"Andrew, sometimes I feel I've moved out of America," Gerald once said.

"This is the real America, Gerald."

"With a caste system that makes India's seem flexible?"

"Savor it, Gerald. It cannot last. What surprises you is that there are considerations other than money that determine rank in the small town."

"Rank! What kind of talk is that? This isn't the army."

"You are confusing easy social mobility based on wealth with a classless society."

"I wondered what I was doing." But they always managed to turn the conversation away from potential disagreements. Andrew had been surprised how easily Gerald settled into Wyler. Among the inducements had been two tournament-level golf courses, one designed by Arnold Palmer, and Andrew's argument that here Gerald could practice the full range of the law.

"You take that job in Chicago and you will be the legal equivalent of the man on the assembly line who turns the same bolt hour after hour, day after day, and hasn't the least idea what goes into making a car."

"Have you been to an automotive assembly plant lately?"

Andrew smiled. "No, I've never been to one. But you know what I mean."

Gerald came to know what Andrew had meant, certainly, and he had become more assimilated than he himself suspected, sharing in Andrew's status at first, but increasingly being seen as deserving of it. And of course there was Julie.

That so lovely a creature should make a man as susceptible to feminine beauty as Andrew Broom scowl was no mystery. Julie was the daughter of Frank McGough, Andrew's rival as the town's leading attorney. Once Gerald had raised his eyebrows at the phrase. The leading attorney in Wyler, Indiana? He was reminded of the remark about Robert Cohn's Princeton boxing title at the beginning of *The Sun Also Rises*.

Since then Gerald had come to have a new understanding of crossing the Rubicon. It was not simply that Andrew preferred being first in Wyler to being second in Chicago—he had been confident that he could have been first there too—but there was all the difference in the world between ascendancy there and ascendancy in Wyler, and he meant professionally.

"You'll be more of a lawyer here, Gerald. An hour's drive will take you to where Lincoln practiced. Think about it."

"How did Jane take it?" Susannah asked.

"She fainted. Literally. Gerald caught her and got her into a chair. I thought for a minute she was going to join Edgar."

"The poor thing. Who's with her?"

"It might not be a bad idea to stop by after lunch."

Susannah had worked for Andrew before they married and after she became his wife there seemed no reason for her to cease being his secretary. There were just Andrew and Gerald, Susannah, and such part-time help as she needed. Emily Nichols had been in the office half a year now, and it was getting harder to think of her as part time.

"Treat her as if she were regular, so far as Social Security and the like goes," Andrew had said.

"Should I ask her to stay on?"

"Sweetheart, that is entirely up to you."

He had half hoped that Emily would catch Gerald's eye, but then he hadn't known she was already spoken for.

Andrew's offices were located on the tenth floor of the Hoosier Towers in Wyler, giving him a magnificent view of the town and surrounding countryside. When he went to the courthouse, as often as not he took the elevator to the basement garage and cut through there to the street and then walked the remaining block and a half. The main reason for this was the presence of the Roundball Lounge on the first floor of the building and the perpetual danger of being waylaid by the chance for edifying conversation.

Today, others got in the elevator on its downward journey, and when the doors opened in the lobby, he stepped out, looking straight ahead as he went by the lounge.

"Andrew Broom," Foster of the *Dealer* said, having just spun through the revolving door from the street. "Got a minute?"

"That depends."

"I'm doing a story on Edgar Bissonet. I understand you discovered the body."

"Not quite."

"You see. You can save me from inaccuracy. Got time for a sip of something?"

They got settled, tasted their beer, and Foster looked around, then hunched forward. "Someone told me you hit the sonofabitch with your drive and that's what killed him."

"Is that the same person who told you I found the body?"

"*Nil nisi bonum de mortuis*, eh?"

"That's on the Pall Mall package, isn't it?"

"You don't have to play country rube with me, Andrew."

"Gerald is the member of the firm who knows Latin."

11

"Seriously?"

"Very seriously." Andrew drank some beer. "You must have a pile of stuff about Edgar, haven't you?"

"I wrote his obituary three years ago. It's a kind of revenge sometimes. A person gets you mad and you go back to your office and write his obituary."

"When did you write mine?"

"The day you married Susannah."

"She'll be delighted to hear that."

"Don't tell her. She never knew I adored her."

"She never even mentioned you."

"Thanks. How long do you suppose it'll take young Matthew to lose everything Edgar gained?"

"Young Matthew."

"Edgar's boy."

"The boy's just turned forty."

Andrew was noncommittal, but he took Fosters point. It might be a good time for investors to go elsewhere than Bissonet Brokers. Of course if a number of people did that, Fosters prediction would be realized without Matthew's lifting a finger.

"You lost some money, Foster?"

"He put me into a mutual fund of Far Eastern growth stocks."

"Did they grow?"

"Sure, but up in China is down here, right?"

"You want an infallible broker, you're out of luck."

"If I want a fallible one, I'll go back to Bissonets."

Andrew turned down the offer of another beer but sat with Foster while he had a second.

"I lead a more stressful life," Foster said.

"Mine isn't stressful at all."

"I can almost believe it."

If the threesome of old guys who had found Edgar

12

Bissonet had been given thought by the experience, Andrew himself had been induced to reflection by the sight of the lifeless body of the broker. Andrew had lost his first wife when she went up in a car fixed to explode when Andrew turned the key. There were very few people who knew that she herself had arranged for the bomb. Whenever he remembered the false medical prognosis that had preceded the explosive end of their marriage, when he had emerged from the clinic after being told that he had only months to live, he could still feel anger at his departed wife. She and her medical lover had falsely told Andrew that he was terminally ill, in the hope that he would take the Stoic route and hasten his own end. And so Andrew had contrived to do, setting in motion a plan for his own execution. When he had learned the diagnosis was rigged, it had been a near thing evading the hit man he himself had hired. In the end, ironically, it was his first wife who had been in the car, and the bomb meant for Andrew had sent her to that bourne from which no traveler returns. But this morning, on the golf course, waiting for the police and paramedics to come for Edgar's body, he'd realized he had a keener sense of life because of that period when he had lived under a death sentence.

Of course he still lived under a death sentence: everyone did.

Quarles the prosecutor came out of his office like a shot when he heard Andrew in his reception room.

"I've been trying to reach you, Andrew. Come in here, will you?"

"I just left my office."

"Well, they said you just left the Roundball."

Quarles closed the door and got Andrew seated

13

before he went behind his desk. He remained standing.

"You were on the course this morning when Edgar was discovered, weren't you?"

"That's right."

"Whelper just told me something I find hard to credit. You know Whelper."

After a long career as a pediatrician, Whelper had announced his candidacy for medical examiner, though no such position existed in Wyler. Whelper argued that it should; there was an ME in all the books he read. Rather than go through the rigmarole of taking up the proposal in the town council, it was thought expedient simply to appoint him medical examiner and attach him to the coroner's office. Ever since he and Evans, the coroner, had been at war.

"What did he say?"

"He doesn't think Edgar died on the golf course. He thinks he had the heart attack and then was carted onto the seventh fairway and put there." Quarles kept a close eye on Andrew as he said this. "You're not laughing."

Andrew remembered that the soles of Edgar's spiked golf shoes had seemed awfully clean, considering the dew and the newly mown grass. But then it was Edgar's habit to drive onto the seventh fairway and start from there, so he wouldn't have done much walking around.

"It's possible."

"My God, what isn't? Did you notice anything funny about the scene?"

"I assume Whelper did."

"He said there was no ball near Edgar. He had a club in his hand but there was no ball."

"That's not very conclusive. I thought he had noticed something else."

"What?"

"The club in Edgar's hand. It was a sand wedge. There was no ball in the sand and if Edgar were going to play the seventh hole with a sand wedge he would shoot a 20."

Quarles stared at him. He sat down. "I can't evaluate that. I don't golf."

"God is merciful."

Andrew was reconstructing in his mind the scene he had come upon this morning after driving off the seventh tee. He and Gerald had hesitated, despite the wild waving on the part of the threesome ahead of them.

"Why don't they move their cart?" Gerald had said.

"They're pulling their clubs."

"Then who belongs to the cart?"

They'd driven their balls and got into the cart and started down the fairway. The three elder statesmen had begun to move toward them. And then Andrew had noticed the body lying on the grass.

The front nine was being mowed this morning, and it was the greenskeeper Gallagher's habit to have his grounds crew begin with the ninth and move back toward the clubhouse and the first hole. Number seven had already been cut; they had passed the lawn mower on five, operated by a girl wearing a baseball cap out of the back of which emerged her ponytail. A liberated woman. There may be sweeter smells than that of a newly mown fairway early in the morning, but Andrew did not know them.

As he recalled the seventh fairway, he could see the paths created by the mower. Were there as well the tracks of Edgar's golf cart, coming from the direction of the house? He looked at his watch. Nearly eleven. He got to his feet.

"What are you going to do?" asked Quarles.

"What I should have done earlier when we found Edgar."

15

THREE

THE MAINTENANCE SHED WAS A LOW FRAME BUILDING set in a hollow behind the second green and across the road from the golf shop. At both the north and south ends of the buildings sliding doors opened so that there was always a contrast, even in the hottest days of summer, between the cool cavelike interior of the building and the sunlit scenes visible through those open doors. The building smelled of grease, spilled oil, gasoline, and rotting grass. Joe Gallagher's office was on the east side, giving him a view of the golf shop from his window.

Joe had come to work at the Wyler Country Club, mowing fairways, aerating greens, this and that, when he was fifteen years old, as a summer job. How it could be called a job was beyond him. He was outdoors all day, he had the fun of riding a wide mower that could turn on a dime and cut to within an inch of the base of a tree, if the operator knew what he was doing. Joe had known what he was doing from the outset, when Mr. Ramsey had singled him out.

"You're a natural, kid," old Ramsey said, and Joe was proud. No one had ever praised him much before.

"A natural grass cutter!" his father said in disbelief.

"John, he's only fifteen. It's a summer job, not a profession," his mother reminded.

But even as a kid Joe knew that it wasn't just a summer job—it wasn't a job at all, he liked it so much. If you like what you're doing, it ain't work, as George Halas was to say, and Joe couldn't agree more.

He worked for Ramsey every summer until he graduated from high school, when he joined the army because he didn't want to wait around and be drafted.

"You're volunteering to go into the army!" said his father.

"John, he'll be drafted sooner or later anyway. He'll get it over with."

He nearly got it over with for good, when his leg was ripped up by enemy fire. He never saw the guy who was shooting at him, never even got a round off himself. He got the Purple Heart and a medical discharge and a disabled pension but most importantly he got his job back at the country club.

"He's lucky they'll take him back," he heard his father tell his mother. He was officially a disabled veteran but to his father he was a cripple lucky to get any job.

They took him on full time, year round, as Ramsey's assistant, and he supervised the kids hired just for summer. Most of them were pretty bad, goofing off, getting out of sight, and parking their mowers and smoking more grass than they cut. Because of the leg, Joe was given a golf cart to get around in, and he found it paid to let the mowers know he might come over any hill at any minute.

Just riding around the course like that, he felt that it was his because just he and Ramsey were responsible for keeping it shipshape. During the winter, he studied so that he had a theory to go along with the practice. He made a point of learning all he could about greens. They had a tendency to dry out and develop dead spots, which didn't affect putting all that much, but they looked bad. By the time Ramsey announced that he was going to retire, the greens looked better than they ever had.

"You're a natural, kid," Ramsey said.

Ramsey didn't live to retirement. He was found out

17

on the course, dead beside the sprinkler he'd been adjusting, the body being regularly watered as the sprinkler came round. That had been on the seventh fairway too, before those houses had been built along it. Finding old Edgar out there this morning had brought back memories of Ramsey, and Joe was sitting in his office, smoking a pipe, not doing much else but thinking when Andrew Broom knocked on the doorframe.

"Busy, Joe?"

Joe got up from his chair, a little embarrassed to be caught just sitting there, but if it had to be any member who surprised him, Andrew Broom would have been his pick. The lawyer looked around the little office.

"How many years has it been since I've been in here?"

"Just don't ask how many years since the first time."

Andrew had grown up on this golf course, but he hadn't been the typical member's kid, the kind that tore up the greens, left unreplaced divots all over the course, and looked right through Joe as if he were invisible. Working late Friday or Saturday nights, Joe would see them boozing it up, throwing one another in the pool, going at in the bushes. Andrew and Joe had been in the same war, but Andrew always dismissed his participation.

"You were down there slogging it out, I just flew over the place."

On the wall behind Joe's desk was a huge picture of Arnie, taken just as he had completed a drive. Andrew pointed to it.

"How he played so well swinging like that is one of the mysteries of the game."

Joe himself had never golfed. He couldn't remember if he had ever swung a club. Andrew beat Wirth two

18

times out of three and played at least four times a week.

"Too bad about old Bissonet," Andrew said.

Joe dropped his chin to his chest.

"Did he start out on the first this morning?"

Joe lifted his head. "You're kidding."

"Just drove his cart onto seven?"

"That's what he usually did. Didn't even tee off. Just drove into the middle of the fairway, dropped a ball, and started. Sometimes there were people on the tee but he just ignored them."

"He's lucky he never got beaned."

"I thought that's what had happened this morning. Until I saw the threesome that found him."

"Gerald and I were behind them. We passed the mower two holes earlier. What time do they start?"

"Same time we always have. Five."

"How long would it take a mower to get from nine to seven?"

"Starting to mow seven? Six-fifteen."

"What do you figure, an hour a hole?"

"It varies of course. Eight is a par three without much fairway to cut."

"So if the mower was on five at eight-thirty, he must have finished seven when?"

"She. That's Patty Cermac doing the front nine this week."

"That's right. The girl with the ponytail."

"She's a natural."

"Blond?"

"That too. Anyway, seven's our longest hole, as I don't have to tell you. She should have finished that at seven-thirty or a little before. You could ask her, if it's important. She might know exactly if she were like the others."

"What do you mean?"

19

"They all listen to the radio or music while they work, earphones clamped over their heads. Hell, I wanted to hear the birds and be where I was. Patty's like me. When she's on the course, her mind is on the course. Still, she might be able to help you."

"I hope so."

"This will fix the time Edgar died?"

Andrew hesitated, but then nodded. "We want to establish how much time elapsed between the mowing of the fairway and the arrival of the threesome of senior citizens."

"And you figure it happened after Patty finished mowing?"

"Unless she mowed around him."

Joe snorted. "She might just as soon mowed right over him. Edgar was a pain in the ass to the grounds crew, Andrew. I don't mind telling you that. I used to wonder how in the world a man like that became a member."

"By marriage, Joe. By marriage."

In the shed, Andrew stopped to look at one of the old mowers that wasn't used much anymore but that Joe kept anyway.

"The blades remind you of a push mower, don't they?" Andrew spun one of the upturned blades and it rotated almost soundlessly. "This is as good as new."

"I used to ride that one."

"Is Patty around now, Joe?"

"She does greens in the afternoon. I've got her on the back nine, the three holes across the road."

FOUR

"YOU GOING DO AN AUTOPSY ON EDGAR?" CECIL Quarles asked Evans, fighting the smell of the doctor's office. Hospitals, examination rooms, pharmacies, even a lavishly furnished medicine cabinet, made him ill. It wasn't fear, it was, he had been told, an allergy. "An allergy to medicine?" he was often asked. "It happens all the time. Some people can't take penicillin. It's the smell I can't take." "Penicillin doesn't have much of a smell." He detected a lack of sympathy. He had never met with much sympathy for his difficulty, so he tried to live with it quietly. Coming to see Evans was a major decision, but this was important.

"Is that an official request?"

"No."

"There's no legal requirement that an autopsy be performed. Mind you, there are ghouls who do them at a drop of a hat. Dying in their jurisdiction is like donating your body to science. Jane want it done?"

"Have you talked with her?"

"About an autopsy?"

"About anything."

"What are you driving at, Cecil?"

"Whelper is saying that Edgar didn't die where he was found but was brought there after his death."

Evans's wrinkled brow continued right on up over his bald head. The lids on his closed eyes were purplish bulges, almost like a sleeping mask. He sighed.

"Whelper is an idiot. Edgar died of a heart attack."

"He spoke to me officially."

"Cecil, he has no official status. He holds a post that

21

doesn't exist. He is a dollar-a-year man, and overpaid at that. Forget what Whelper says."

"Would you give me that in writing?"

Evans blew up. He pushed back from his desk and paced up and down, his open cloth jacket whirling as he turned. "If I started writing out denials of what Whelper says I'd be doing nothing else. He *looks* for trouble."

"He says the body had rigor mortis so bad it couldn't be that Edgar died just before he was found."

Evans threw up his hands. "Okay. You want an autopsy, ask me in writing."

"Aw, Art."

"Don't Art me, Mr. Quarles. We're going to behave like this, let's keep it formal."

"Andrew Broom thought Whelper had a point. Something about the golf club he was gripping. The particular one it was. A wedge?"

Quarles could see that Andrew's apparent openness to what Whelper suggested had given Evans pause. He sat at his desk and put a huge hand on top of his head. He brought it down over his face and a tragic mask became a comic one. Art must have been great with his grandchildren. "I'll do it," he whispered.

"I think we ought to play it safe, don't you?"

"Like Edgar, maybe. Sure he was holding a wedge, but he could have just been playing it safe. Seven is the longest hole on the course, a par five. I try to keep it in single digits, it's that hard for me. I have sworn I could par the damned thing just hitting seven irons. Maybe Edgar told himself he could do it with a wedge."

"I don't play golf."

"No wonder you're so jumpy."

Quarles felt good when he left Evans's office, to escape the medicinal smell and because of what he had accomplished. Alex, Quarles's third son, had an understanding with Alyson Spencer, the granddaughter of Jane Spencer Bissonet's deceased brother George. Anything that might jeopardize union with a family like the Spencers was anathema to Quarles. He had gone to see Art Evans to put a flea in his ear and hoped the coroner would act professionally. Who would think the prosecutor had been involved in the decision to have an autopsy?

He returned to the courthouse content with himself. Whelper had come to him earlier with gleaming eye, clearly suggesting that there was something amiss with Edgar's death and that it would eventually land on the prosecutor's desk. The volunteer medical officer might be an idiot, but Quarles didn't want anyone saying he neglected his duties. Now there would be an autopsy, but any objection to its being done, and people can be touchy about autopsies, would have to be directed to Evans. It seemed a good day's work.

Until he got the call from Matthew Bissonet.

"What is this nonsense about an autopsy, Cecil?"

"Evans has decided to do one."

"He says at your suggestion."

"My suggestion?" His laugh would not have gained him a place in a live studio audience. "I passed on to him some remarks of Dr. Whelper and Andrew Broom."

"Andrew Broom!"

"He was there when your father's body was found."

That was the end of that conversation. And Quarles thought that he had deflected any family discontent to Evans and Whelper—where it belonged. It would not do

23

to have the son of the great-uncle of his future daughter-in-law bearing a grudge against him. Then it occurred to Quarles that the events of the morning had most likely made Matthew Bissonet closer to being a very wealthy man.

Meanwhile, Quarles telephoned Andrew's office and left a message with Susannah that Evans had decided to go ahead with an autopsy on Edgar Bissonet. If shivering has a sound he heard it then.

"I'll tell him, Cecil," Susannah said. "How are plans for the big wedding going?"

"I just hope recent events don't throw a monkey wrench into the machinery."

"What are you talking about?"

"Edgar Bissonet was the uncle of the bride-to-be," Quarles said solemnly.

"Cecil, that's nonsense. Even if the wedding were this Saturday, it would still take place. Besides, wasn't Edgar her great-uncle?"

"That's what I meant."

"And you think his death would interfere with the wedding of those young people? Cecil, where have you been all these years?"

"Don't forget. They're Spencers."

"And you know what we used to chant when we were kids: Spencers hold up pants but Evans won't let you down."

Cecil Quarles laughed the laugh of one who hopes he isn't being overheard. "I'd forgotten that. The autopsy was Dr. Whelper's idea, the old idiot."

"Now, just a minute. He delivered me."

"He thinks Edgar died and then someone carted him out onto the fairway to be found there."

"Why would anyone do that?"

"He didn't say. Andrew seemed to think it might have happened that way."

"He did?"

"Edgar was holding a wedgie."

"A woman's shoe?"

"No, a golf club. Widgie, wedgie."

"Wedge!" Susannah said. She had a pretty laugh, even on the telephone.

Sheriff Cleary was seated behind his desk with his arms folded, his eyes shut, and his lips moving. Quarles stopped. Had he surprised the sheriff at prayer? He began to back out of the office but banged into the coatrack and damned near threw his back out catching it before it hit the floor.

"May I cut in?" Cleary said.

"I got it before it hit the floor," Quarles said, restoring the rack to its place.

"You looked like you were doing the dip. Remember those dances at the Showboat down the river at Mullertown?"

"Remember? We still go."

"What brings you over?"

"Edgar Bissonet."

Cleary sat forward, uttering with great precision an uncharacteristic obscenity.

"Edgar was a pain in the butt alive and I predict he's going to be more trouble dead."

"Why do you say that?"

"Whelper examined the body and says it wasn't a heart attack that killed him but asphyxiation."

"Cecil, we're going to have to do something about Whelper. He is hyperactive and underemployed. The council has got to dissolve that nothing job and put

Whelper back to pasture."

"He seems pretty certain there's something fishy with Edgar's death."

Cleary shook his head. "People swear he was a good baby doctor. Why did he have to grow up?"

"What were you doing when I came in?"

"Reviewing the case for not going out to the Bissonets."

"Weren't you out there this morning to see the body on the ground."

Cleary nodded. "And I saw what I went out to see. An old geezer who'd had the big one while playing his last round of golf. But maybe Whelper's right."

"You been talking to Andrew Broom?"

"He called, yes."

"I thought so."

Cleary got up and stretched, exhibiting the damp underarms of his uniform shirt. "Want to come along out there with me?"

"The sheriff and the prosecutor knocking at their door? Hell no."

FIVE

ANDREW TOOK A GOLF CART OUT ONTO THE COURSE TO talk with Patty Cermac, although it was now going on noon.

"She has her lunch out there," Gallagher said. "She's a loner."

Andrew directed the soundless electric cart along the paths provided on the edges of the fairways, but at the third hole, he cut through the fairway and went on a more direct line for the bridge that would take him

26

across the road to fifteen, sixteen, and seventeen, three of the best holes on the course. They were the least changed of any of the holes since he was a kid, so going over the bridge was a little like leaving the present behind and going into the past.

He eased up on the pedal, bringing the cart to a stop on the crest of the arching bridge, and looked through the screened guard at the traffic passing below. Whenever he looked down at the cars hurtling north and south he would be even more thankful that he was on the course.

"How do you ever get any work done?" Gerald had asked.

"I won't say I get it done on the course. I never talk business when I golf. But in some sense, my mind is working away while I'm concentrating on the game."

He contrasted for Gerald what the consumption of time would be in Chicago if he golfed this much. The travel back and forth to the course would equal the time he actually spent on the course in Wyler. And what was the point of a relaxing game if you had to plunge into hair-raising traffic right afterward? You got home or back to the office in worse shape than before the game.

"You're protesting too much."

"Maybe. But this is the way I live my life, and God willing it's the way I'll go on living it."

"Hey, I'm not criticizing."

"Sure you are. Gerald, you've still to pick up the basic rhythm of Wyler."

"I'm working on it," Gerald said, clasping his hands and taking back an imaginary club.

"You're corrupting youth," Susannah said, half seriously. "You've devised a way of living that includes scads of hard work. Gerald might come to see the work as interfering with the golf."

"And he complains that I keep him too busy."

"You're just trying to reduce the chances of his seeing Julie."

He pressed the golf cart pedal and came down on the opposite side of the road. There were only two foursomes on this portion of the course. And he could see the mower parked under a huge willow and a figure seated under the tree, back against its bole.

As he got nearer, he saw that Patty was having her lunch, and he felt bad about interrupting her. On the other hand, it would have been hard to interview her while she was mowing. She was watching him approach, chewing a sandwich, one hand on a can of Coke on the ground next to her.

"I'm Andrew Broom," he said, coming to a stop a few feet from her. He decided to remain in the cart.

Her mouth was full, but she nodded and said, "I know."

"I'm on the course a lot."

"If I played that well I'd play a lot too."

"Do you play?"

A shrug. "Sort of."

"Where?"

"Here, on Monday mornings. Joe lets me make up the time."

Monday morning was always slow. Years ago, when there had been caddies, that was the morning the caddies were allowed to play the course. Maybe that's what Joe was remembering.

"I'd like to play with you sometime."

She shook her head. "Not till I'm better."

She had a smooth tanned face and eyes that looked steadily at him. There was no coquetry, damned little to indicate she was a female, really. A tomboy, she would

28

have been called once, and there was the suggestion of Huck Finn about her. The free spirit. She had removed her shoes and her toes moved around in the cool grass as she sat there.

"You're going to get better?"

"I'm going to get good."

He liked that. If you were going to do a thing, do it well.

"I want to ask you some questions about the old man who was found dead on the seventh fairway this morning."

"You're a lawyer, aren't you?"

"Yes. But I'm asking these questions on my own, and as a member of the club. When did you begin mowing seven?"

Again the shrug. "I don't wear a watch."

"Joe figures it would have been about seven."

"I suppose so. He would know."

"Why don't you wear a watch?"

"A leather band is too hot and a metal band pinches."

It seemed to underscore the carefree life she led. What difference did it make what time it was?

"Did you ever read Thoreau?"

The question startled him. *"Walden Pond?"*

"In it he tells of the coming of time to small towns. The railroad brought it. Trains left at a given time, and arrived at a given time, and the hoots and whistles and clocks on the depot changed what a day was for Americans.

"You prefer to live by the sun?"

"And by the noon whistle." Her smile showed teeth made whiter by her tanned skin. "That's how I know it's lunchtime."

"You didn't notice the old man come on the course, did you?"

"He was sitting on his patio when I mowed seven. I waved to him."

"You did?"

"I supposed he was waiting for me to finish. But it wasn't until I was on five that he did."

"You saw him drive onto seven?"

"I saw his cart come from the house and stop where they found it. It was still a little hazy so I couldn't see too well. It looked as if he were carrying an extra bag of clubs."

"How so?"

"There was a bag strapped to the back." She pointed at the cart Andrew was on. There was a low shelf in back, room for two bags to be strapped on.

"He had two bags back here?"

"No. The other was sort of lying across the cart, behind the seat."

"What else."

"Then I had to turn and mow back the other way. When I turned again, the cart was standing there, but there was only one bag of clubs."

"Any sign of Edgar?"

"By that time those three old guys were on the tee. I thought it was the extra bag lying next to the cart."

"That was Edgar."

"So Joe told me. Poor old guy."

"Did you know him at all."

"Sort of. He liked to talk. And he had an eye, the way old men sometimes do, you know. Flirting away, because they know you won't take them seriously."

Andrew found it hard to imagine Edgar Bissonet flirting, but then it is difficult to imagine others in the grips of sexual folly at any age.

"What do you think happened, Patty?"

30

She had peeled an orange and was eating it section by section. She leaned forward to spit out some seeds.

"Someone drove him onto the course and dumped him there beside the cart. His body must have been what I thought was a second bag."

"What did the driver look like?"

"Since I thought it was Mr. Bissonet, it looked like him."

"You didn't see the other man when he left the cart?"

"I didn't say it was a man."

"That's right, you didn't."

"At first I thought it was him, the old man, but the way he dressed for golf, a real Christmas tree, it could have been a woman too I guess."

"It's odd you would think that."

"No. Sometimes I'd see him sitting in his yard with a woman."

"His wife?"

"Is she a lot younger than he is?"

"No.

"This was a young woman."

"And you think she might have driven him onto the seventh fairway this morning?"

"I don't think that, no. But I can't say for sure it was a man at the wheel of the cart."

"You'd make a good witness, Patty."

"In court? I'd be too nervous to say anything."

Nervous. He couldn't imagine her nervous. But she was in her environment now. What had Joe said? She's a natural.

"Is there going to be a trial?"

Andrew realized that the question had been on the edge of consciousness for a number of hours now. Whelper might be an imaginative old fool, but he was

31

also a doctor who had been highly esteemed during his active years. And now there was this straightforward talk from Patty. At the moment it looked as if a whole lot could depend on her testimony if there was a trial. But he saw no reason to get her upset.

"We'll see. Thanks a lot, Patty. I have a better picture now of what happened."

"Don't forget about golfing with me."

"Let me know when you're ready."

He pressed down on the pedal and made a wide lazy circle and started back toward the bridge. Why didn't Gerald fall in love with a natural like Patty? If she ever did challenge him to a Monday morning round, he'd bring Gerald along.

Six

WHEN SUSANNAH ARRIVED AT THE BISSONET HOUSE AT two that afternoon, the family had begun to gather and Susannah hesitated before going in. Andrew had said that Jane had fainted that morning when she learned Edgar had been found dead on the golf course. That was not at all the kind of reaction one would have expected from one of the most esteemed matriarchs in Wyler. And now, surrounded by children and grandchildren and in-laws, Jane looked very much in charge of the situation.

"Susannah," she said simply when she saw her and held out her hand.

Susannah went to Jane, bent over, and embraced her. It seemed best to say nothing, since the things one did say on such occasions were always so idiotic.

"I don't know what I would have done if Andrew and Gerald hadn't been here this morning. Those three old fools Abner, Bullock, and McCoy kept jabbering away about what a nice way it was to go, on the golf course. We all but live on the course, so that scarcely seems a significant mark of Edgar's going."

"Did he golf every day, Jane?"

"The fact is, he talked about it more than he did it. Where he was found is just off our yard and by and large he would just hit balls around there, annoying the players who were having a real game."

"Did you see him go onto the course today?"

Jane looked up at her. "Why do you ask?"

"I think you should prepare yourself for what Whelper is telling anyone who will listen. He thinks Edgar didn't die on the course."

"Of course he did. That's where they found him."

"That is not in question. But had he died earlier and then . . ."

"What nonsense. People say Dr. Whelper has only become eccentric since he retired. That's not so. I wouldn't have him deliver my children, the girls or Matthew. I had an appointment with him when I was expecting Harriet and I decided never to go back to him. Obstetrics was a license for him to speak suggestively to women." Jane leaned forward and Susannah bowed to hear her whisper, "He told me of the pleasure I would have nursing the baby. Widening his eyes as he said it. Heavens knows it's fulfilling for a mother to nurse her child, but he was suggesting something else."

Susannah, who had never had children, didn't know quite what to say to that.

"Why, here's Andrew Broom," someone said and there he was indeed. He looked solemn and bowed and shook hands as he moved toward Susannah and Jane.

33

"You're going to have to put up with a lot of busybody visitors, Jane."

"I was just telling Susannah what a good thing it was that you were here this morning."

"Has Susannah told you about Whelper's claim?"

"Can I sue him if he keeps spreading such a rumor?"

Andrew looked at Susannah and she could see he had learned something relevant to Whelper's theory.

"Jane, is there somewhere private we could talk?"

She studied his face and saw there what Susannah had seen.

"We can go down to Edgar's study. God knows we won't be heard down there."

From the front, the house was a single story, but in the back, because of the contour of the lot, it was two stories and Edgar had a room flush with the back lawn. A miniature escalator, which could be made to go up or down, took them to ground level. They came into a large all-purpose room with a great fireplace and comfortable furniture, including a massive television set. The room was separated by sliding doors from an outside patio. Edgar's study opened off this room.

"I suppose we could talk here," Jane said, indicating the all-purpose room.

"Could I see Edgar's study?"

A shadow passed over Jane's face. "It just occurred to me that he'll never use it again."

Susannah took Jane's hand and Andrew went to open the study door. Unsuccessfully. He tried again.

"It seems to be locked."

"Of course it is. What am I thinking? It was a fetish of his to keep that room sacrosanct. Feel above the doorframe and see if there isn't a key."

Andrew felt along the upper frame until his fingers came upon a key.

"Isn't that the first place you'd look? Edgar would have had to stand on a chair to get it, so he thought it was out of everyone's reach."

Andrew fitted the key in the lock and turned it.

"There's a switch just inside, to the right."

He felt for it and flicked it on and found himself looking at a room that someone had torn to pieces.

"My God in heaven," Jane cried, pushing past Andrew. "What has happened here? Oh, look at it, look at it." She raised her anguished face to Andrew. "He kept this place as neat as a pin. If he saw it like this it would kill him."

Her mouth fell open when she realized what she had said. Then she turned to Susannah and was taken into her arms. Andrew indicated to his wife that she should take Jane back into the all-purpose room. He turned off the study light and closed and locked the door.

Susannah had Jane sit on a sofa and then she and Andrew sat on either side of her.

"Jane, this seems an awful time to go into this, but it won't get easier, so I'm going to tell you what we have to do. First, the girl who mows the fairways saw someone drive Edgar's cart onto the golf course this morning. Edgar was lying in back, between the seat and his bag of clubs. Like it or not, it looks as if Whelper is right."

Jane took her lower lip between her teeth, trying to adjust to this dreadful news.

"I locked the study again. Obviously something went on in there. It could be where Edgar died."

A little cry escaped Jane, and Susannah put her arm around the old woman's shoulders again.

"I am going to contact the IBI in Indiana, after talking with Sheriff Cleary, of course. Some professionals will go over that room and see what it can tell us about what happened to Edgar."

"You're saying that someone killed him?"

"I am suggesting that it is possible. It seems certain that he died before he was taken onto the golf course. Was anyone else in the house besides yourself?"

"Andrew, there could have been an army of people in that study and I wouldn't have known."

"You sleep that soundly?"

She laughed a sad little laugh. "Andrew's study is soundproof. Did you notice the single bed? He slept there. Since the second year of our marriage, we have slept in different bedrooms, and his had to be soundproof."

"Why?"

Jane looked at Susannah and then at Andrew. "He snored. Terribly. From one end of the night to the other. At first, it didn't bother me, but very soon it threatened to ruin our marriage. I don't think there is anything that alters your attitude more toward another person than snoring." She shuddered. "Of course it wasn't his fault, but when you are wakened night after night to the incessant sound of snoring, it seems intentional, as if it were meant to aggravate you and keep you awake."

"Aren't there cures for snoring?"

"There are promised cures. They are very much like claims to bring hair back to a bald head. We tried them all. Edgar even had an operation on his nose. He continued to snore. There were various devices meant to keep him off his back, but Edgar snored on both sides as well as facedown."

"Jane, how awful." But Susannah looked as if she might laugh.

"And of course I tried earplugs of various kinds. Hypnotism hadn't worked for him and it didn't work for me either. I was supposed to not hear the snoring after I was hypnotized. But Edgar's snoring broke through any psychic block."

"So you slept in separate rooms."

"There wasn't anything wrong with our marriage," Jane said delicately. "The trouble began after Edgar fell asleep. But separate bedrooms did not solve it. Inevitably the penetrating drone of his snoring would wake me, and though it was better than having him in the same bed beside me, it made it impossible for me to sleep. Then someone told Edgar of Marcel Proust's cork-lined room. Well, there is better soundproofing than cork now, and Edgar shopped around until he had the best. I can't tell you how heavenly it was not to hear him snore."

When they'd built this house, a soundproof room for Edgar had been one of the instructions given to the architect.

"So someone could have been in there with him this morning and you would not have known."

"No."

"But wouldn't you have seen someone go in?"

"I didn't."

"All the more reason why that room has to be gone over carefully. Is this the only key?"

"Edgar had one, of course."

Andrew would be able to check with Evans and see what had been done with the clothes Edgar had been wearing and the contents of his pockets.

"So this is where you are," said Claire, Matthew Bissonet's wife. "Am I interrupting legal business?"

Susannah knew that when Andrew closed his small

37

account with Edgar, Edgar had dropped him as a lawyer, tit for tat, and worse, had made a point of letting it be known that he was now a client of Frank McGough.

Susannah apologized to Claire for monopolizing Jane but said that she and Andrew wanted to be of any help they could.

"But not legal help," Andrew said, and Susannah at least could detect the edge to his voice.

"But I want your legal help, Andrew," Jane said.

Susannah marveled at the way he could bow and smile and seem to respond but really not commit himself to anything. He had not needed Edgar's business, but it had angered him when Edgar went elsewhere for a lawyer.

"You did the same thing to him," Susannah had said.

"No, I didn't. I did not turn to another broker. I began to manage my own investments via the computer. There is a broker's fee, but there isn't another person I replaced Edgar with."

He had obviously spent some time establishing to his own satisfaction the dissimilarity between Edgar's deed and his own. Susannah hoped now that he wouldn't punish Jane for what Edgar had done.

She and Claire took Jane up to the others, but Andrew stayed behind. Would he, despite what he said to Jane, take a look around the study? Or did he just want to survey the route Edgar would have taken from the metal shed in which he kept his golf cart to the fairway?

"It's so good to have Andrew to rely on," Jane said as they went up the little escalator.

"Where is Matthew?" Claire asked.

"I wish somebody would get hold of him. I know he can't just drop everything, but after all . . ."

38

SEVEN

WHEN GERALD CAME BACK TO THE OFFICE HE FOUND the place wide open but there was no sign of either Andrew or Susannah. It was the latter rather than the former that surprised him—in Wyler, his uncle had informed him in his ongoing orientation course into Midwest small-town living, in Wyler we do not lock doors—or our houses, or our cars. Not uniformly true, of course, but close enough to underscore the difference between Gerald's lifestyle and the multiple locks, alarms, and security systems of his former classmates who had made the smart career move, were on the bottom rungs of firms in Chicago, LA, or New York, and lived in circumstances similar to those of guerrillas engaged in jungle combat.

There was a cup half full of still-warm coffee on Emily's desk. Gerald went into Andrew's office and looked at the town and the country beyond. Even on an overcast day, you could see forever out here. His eye still longed to be impeded by a mountain, but he had to confess he was learning to like flatness more and more. Of course he had just come from lunch with Julie, who was anything but flat.

"The truck stop?" she had said, the first time he suggested they meet there.

"How many of your friends go there?"

"I don't know. Let's find out."

It had become their rendezvous.

"People don't have rendezvous in Wyler."

"Julie, I am relatively new here and I could tell you stories if it weren't for professional confidentiality."

"Is that what people talk to lawyers about?"

"Ask your father."

A frown. It was wrong to allude to her paternal parent, just as mention of his uncle Andrew was a reminder that the two people who really mattered most to each of them were adamantly opposed to their knowing one another, let alone anything further. The impropriety of their affair added zest to their love and had led to the discovery of interesting places like the truck stop, but ultimately it amounted to a massive veto. They lived in the hope of removing it and dreaded the eventual need to act contrary to the wishes of Andrew Broom and Frank McGough.

"What is it with those two, Julie? Really."

"It's all your uncle's fault, or so I'm told."

"And I'm told it's your father's."

No point in mentioning that he shared Andrew's dislike for the booming-voiced, flamboyant, backslapping Frank McGough, whose finger was in all the wrong pies.

Elsewhere, young people lived together without benefit of matrimony, but not in Wyler. Elsewhere, young people might anticipate conjugal joys on a more regular basis, sometimes with a variety of partners, but not in Wyler. Elsewhere, young adults could decide whom to marry and then inform their families on the assumption that their choice would be accepted because it was theirs, but not in Wyler.

"Marriage is a tribal act, Gerald, not just a private agreement."

He hated the effect of all this on the two of them while at the same time liking more and more the atmosphere that produced it. But he always returned from lunch with Julie expecting a complicit smile from Susannah and suspicion from Andrew. And today he

40

found neither. Not even Emily was in evidence.

He went into his office, sighing, deciding someone had to do some work, and had just slipped out of his jacket when Emily came in.

"Did Andrew call again?" she asked.

He spread his hands and looked around his desk. "I don't see the message."

"I was just down the hall," she said petulantly.

"Andrew called?"

She drew back her shoulders, stared at the ceiling, and said, in a recitative tone, "He and Susannah are at the Bissonets', Matthew is not there, would you please find him?" She dropped her eyes and smiled.

"Thank you."

"I didn't realize that you and Andrew had found the body."

"Not quite. There was a threesome ahead of us who found him."

"But you saw him?"

"Yes."

"Dead?" Her eyes grew large. What did she imagine Edgar had looked like?

"Very. Stiff as a board."

Bissonet Brokers was in the Hoosier Towers, four floors down, and Gerald took the stairway, for exercise and to save time. The girl in the outer office looked up receptively, as if he had come to see her.

"Matthew in?"

"Yes, Mr. Broom."

"Rowan. Gerald Rowan."

"But aren't you Mr. Broom's nephew?"

"Yes. But . . ."

Her expression had grown more receptive and she

41

leaned toward him, with interesting results. Her questions were ploys. Why had he been so smitten by the forbidden Julie, when such ripe fruit as Emily and this nubile receptionist seemed to hang from every branch in town?

Matthew Bissonet, tall, harried, rumpled, his hair fallen over his forehead, looked out of his office.

"Gerald. I thought I heard your voice. I'm trying to catch up on things so I can ignore this place for a few days, which is impossible. Both catching up and ignoring it."

"Some tickers never stop."

Matt thought about it, then nodded. "My mother said you and Andrew were a great help this morning."

"He and Susannah are with her now."

"Oh God. The house is already full of relatives. I slipped away . . ."

Doubtless Matthew's manner was in part due to the fact that he had just lost his father and was finding it difficult to leave the concerns of his office and go to his mother. But as a general rule, Gerald found Matthew's manner to be one that would not encourage confidence in a potential client.

"Claire is there, of course."

"Of course."

"The market will close in half an hour."

If nothing else, Matthew ran a high-tech operation. There were several people sitting in a little theaterlike room, watching the quotes sail past. Were they investors or just watchers?

"Why don't I come back when it does close? We can go out to the house together."

"Fine. Good." He turned to take a slip from young Trumble, who looked the way a broker should, neat, smug,

42

on top of the world. He nodded to Gerald, and remained after Matthew took the note and dashed into his office.

"The Tokyo market," he said.

"Ah so."

"Did you play golf this morning?"

"Is Dan Quayle a Hoosier?"

Trumble adopted an expression of envy, but somehow Gerald thought Trumble preferred getting up here to the electronic gadgetry, the phones, the portfolios, as soon as possible in the morning.

"What time do you start work in the morning, Stan?"

"Ideally, we should never close. The markets never do. They overlap around the world and trades can be made around the clock."

"Do you deal in all markets?"

"Is there something you're particularly interested in?"

That was what he liked about Trumble, he was always on the lookout for clients, without being pushy. Gerald had considered opening an account, a small account, with Bissonet Brokers but if he did he would want to be Trumble's client, and he wasn't sure that was the way it would work out. Trumble had suggested, oh so obliquely, that without the bumbling incompetence of Matthew Bissonet he could have this brokerage humming in a matter of weeks, but that was the usual attitude of the hireling.

"Bad news about the founder," Trumble said.

"Yes."

"You found the body?"

Precision on this matter seemed picky. "We found the founder."

"Who foundered on the fairway." A flickering little smile. Trumble did the Sunday *Times* crossword with a ballpoint pen and left it completed, erasure free, lying about on Monday mornings, an ambiguous rebuke to Matthew.

"Edgar didn't come in anymore, did he?"

Trumble glanced toward Matthew's office. "A cup of coffee? Good idea." He steered Gerald past the receptive receptionist and into the hall. "Do you have coffee upstairs? Louella has never mastered the intricacies of Mr. Coffee. It's the only mister that doesn't interest her."

"Let's go found out."

"I don't care if you do or not," Trumble said in the elevator. "I could have cheered when you said you were going to take Matthew away after New York closes. He has been screwing things up all day."

Gerald took Trumble into Andrew's office.

"When did he hear about his father?"

"Before he came in, I guess. It was after ten when he showed up. I had already heard about Edgar and assumed Matthew wouldn't be coming in at all. I mean, he shouldn't have. His mother is old and all alone in that house." Trumble shook his head. "But he has convinced himself that he must have a hand in everything. That is annoying enough on ordinary days, but today he has been absolutely useless."

"I suppose it hit him hard."

Trumble shrugged. "Who knows what he feels? If anything. Of course he and Edgar had quarreled. And the old man was in the right. Bissonet Brokers is not what it was or what it should be."

"Well, I suppose with the economy . . ."

"Bunk. One has to be on the alert of course, but one can always make money for clients. Always."

"But potential investors should be advised that past performance . . ."

Trumble waved away the conventional disclaimer. "I assure them they will make money. If not here, there, if not with stocks, bonds, domestic, foreign—the potential has never been so vast. We should be flourishing. But Matthew adopts that Miniver Cheevy expression and warns about risks."

"Who is Miniver Cheevy?"

"Edwin Arlington Robinson."

"A pseudonym?"

"One of his poems."

Gerald got the point, but he didn't want to encourage Trumble to go on like this about his employer.

"How long do you plan to stay with him?"

Trumble's expression became one of mild alarm. "What have you heard?"

"I would rather hear it from you."

"Bankers. They're town criers."

But that was all. If Stan Trumble set up a rival brokerage, it could deliver the final coup de grace to the Bissonet Brokers.

Gerald got back to his office where he found Andrew and Susannah returned. Susannah was telling Emily who had been at the Bissonets.

"I'll go to the wake," Emily said.

"Do you know the family?" Susannah asked.

"Well, everyone knows the Bissonets and the Spencers. But Chuckie Spencer and I used to date, so I feel an obligation." She rolled her eyes expressively at Gerald as she said this.

Gerald closed Andrew's door behind him and reported that Matthew Bissonet had not shown up at his office until after ten, he was more of a nervous wreck than usual, if he didn't watch out Trumble would set up a rival brokerage, and he had a receptionist they ought to snap up in case the brokerage folded.

"One of the deserving poor?" Andrew asked.

"Have you ever seen her?"

"I know her father, Gerald. That tends to quiet the libido."

"What do you think about Matthew?"

"That someone is bound to ask him what he was doing until after ten this morning."

Matthew had a home a few doors away from his parents, one he had built despite the lack of enthusiasm of either of his parents to have him that close. Besides, it irked Edgar that his son's first house should be on a par with the one in which he dwelled after a stellar career.

"That puts him right in the vicinity," Gerald said.

"There were a good many people right in the vicinity. And there is one known eyewitness."

"Who?"

"The girl who mowed the front nine. She saw what turns out to have been someone else carting Edgar's body onto the course."

"Could she identify him?"

"I don't know. It occurs to me that we should resume a low profile in this investigation. Increasingly, it looks as if someone is going to be accused of killing Edgar."

"And you might represent him?"

"Or you might represent her."

"Her who?"

"Her is not a proper name."

"Frank McGough succeeded you as Edgar's lawyer, didn't he?"

Andrew looked sharply at Gerald. "Are you suggesting that a member of his family might have done it?"

"Maybe another member of the family will become your client."

Gerald could see that Andrew was getting revved up, eager to get into a courtroom with something as juicy as a murder trial. And if it was going to involve one of the most prominent families in town, he definitely wanted to be defense counsel.

"You've always told me that most murderers are either close relatives or lovers of the victim."

"That's true."

"That's all I meant."

"It will probably turn out to have a perfectly innocent and plausible explanation," Andrew said, but it was not his most persuasive tone of voice.

EIGHT

JACK WIRTH HAD WANTED TO BE A BASEBALL PLAYER, but people kept telling him he was a better golfer. For a while he did both, playing single A ball and entering as many amateur golf tournaments as he could. Once he qualified for the Open from Indiana, and that decided him, but in his heart of hearts he still considered himself a ballplayer. Of course if he had gone into baseball, he would be retired now and sitting in Arizona or Florida nursing his aching limbs in the sun. At least golf was a game you can play until you drop.

Joe Gallagher told him Andrew Broom had talked to the girl who had mowed the fairways on the front nine. The simple explanation—that Edgar had died of a heart attack—had been called into question.

"He was out there when they found Edgar," Joe said. "I went out there when the ambulance came and

Andrew and his nephew were still there. I guess he wanted to know if Patty noticed anything."

"You mean saw him fall over?"

Joe shrugged. "She told me she hadn't been of much help to him."

"What's he looking for?"

But Joe was through talking. Ask him about something specific, the machinery, the need for a new roof on the maintenance shed, the drainage on the fourteenth green, and he would tell you all you needed to know. But he had no gift for general talk, meaning, Jack supposed, gossip.

Sheriff Cleary came out with his Stetson set level on his head and spent an hour with Abner, Bullock, and McCoy in the bar. The threesome had been in there since their round had been interrupted, ordering club sandwiches for lunch, but basically drinking beer. Cleary refused a beer but accepted a Coke with a wink in it, a wink of bourbon.

Bruce Hutton, who worked in the pro shop, was told by the bartender that the old geezers had given Cleary a line of bull about what they had seen.

"Bullock said he fell over like a felled tree, he kept repeating that phrase, a felled tree. Hasn't a felled tree already fallen?"

"Better ask Dr. Bullock."

"His wife came and took him home."

The threesome had described in great detail what they assumed happened, getting more and more colorful as they went on. That's when Cleary told them there was reason to believe Edgar had died before he was put on the fairway.

"Why'd he say that?"

"I guess Edgar was stiff as a board and that doesn't happen until you've been dead for a while."

48

Wirth hated talk about death. He was now forty-nine years old, in his fiftieth year, when you stopped to think of it, and had begun to realize how ancient he seemed to the young. And it was getting harder to see old people as if they were a separate race. Jack was developing arthritis in his hands, although he had told no one. A golf pro with arthritis is not going to be of much help to anyone.

"McCoy tried to alter his testimony to accommodate this new hypothesis, but he was already discredited."

Jack indicated that Bruce could get back to work. The golf shop was a very lucrative part of Jack Wirth's income—giving lessons, selling equipment, keeping the members' clubs in good order, featuring a line of clothes that was absurdly overpriced but moved pretty well. Edgar had been a good customer, the gaudier the attire the better. It was a way to get back some of the money he had lost as Edgar's client.

"I advised against buying that stock," Edgar would say.

"Advised against it?"

"Look at its record."

"It's no worse than the stocks you do recommend."

"Maybe so. But I only take the blame for my own mistakes."

Jack knew it was ridiculous to second-guess his own broker. He knew what he would have thought of someone who took lessons from him and then insisted on doing things his own way. But Edgar was so conservative and Jack wanted money, lots of it. After Edgar retired but kept Jack as a client, his prospects had never looked better and his money should really have grown. His money. He didn't have much to show for a lifetime spent kowtowing to the rich. He had been as bad a client as Edgar was a student.

49

The worse the player, the more likely he was to imagine that he swung like one of the better pros. Edgar should have won trophies as the worst golfer in the state. It was difficult for Jack to understand what pleasure a man could get out of playing that poorly.

Edgar may have dressed like a clown and swung like a woman but it was best to treat him with complete seriousness. Jack was always serious when he gave lessons, but that was not easy with Edgar, who was essentially unteachable. But the man had the Midas touch.

"I'll make you rich," Edgar had said years ago, and he was perfectly serious. "You give me ten thousand more each year and by the time you're fifty you'll have as much money as most of the members."

Jack didn't have ten thousand dollars then and when he did turn to Edgar he tried to speed up the process, making his own trades, interfering with his broker. And now he was past the age when Edgar had said he could be rich.

Jack and his wife lived in one of the houses built along the seventh fairway, but they didn't own it. It was built for the club pro and considered part of his compensation to live in it rent-free. Mona, who was totally and completely unathletic, looked the gift horse in the mouth and had her doubts.

"Jack, you'll never get away from your job."

"It's rent-free, Mona. Do you know what that means annually?"

"What difference will it make? You'll just want to save it and I'll never see it."

"Of course we'll save it."

It was painful to think what that would have amounted to by now if he had just put it in certificates of deposit. But it became a sum with which he opened an account with Bissonet Brokers.

"You always make fun of Edgar," Mona said.

"As a golfer, sure." He had told her that his bad luck in the market was due to following Edgar's advice. Sometimes he himself believed this was true.

Edgar might be old and physically a wreck, but his mind was clear. He had more time to devote to Jack now that he was retired. That was when Jack had turned almost everything over to Edgar.

"I'll do it as a favor, in gratitude for what you've done for my game."

"Don't mention it, Edgar."

And he meant it. He hated to bear any responsibility for the way Edgar Bissonet played golf. And he hated to think what he might be worth now if he had just left everything in Edgar's hands without interfering. Now he would have to recoup his losses on his own.

Wirth was due home for dinner at six-thirty but he left Bruce in charge, hopped into a golf cart, and headed across the course. He did not go in a straight line, but followed a circuitous route, keeping to the cart paths, trying not to attract the attention of the golfers. Invariably, they wanted some instant instruction. Doctors were the worst, yet he had heard them discuss in pretty harsh terms people who tried to get a consultation at a social meeting.

He answered hallos with a wave and kept his foot on the pedal. An electric golf cart is the quietest machine on earth; put it on the grass and it is even quieter. He approached his house from the farthest point on the course, bringing the cart right up to the edge of the patio without making a sound. He was wearing a pair of the lounging shoes he was pushing in the golf shop, rubber soles, as silent as the machine. He eased the sliding door back very carefully, just wide enough to step through.

He heard the television on upstairs, but he ignored it and moved quietly down the hall and looked into all the bedrooms. Only then did he go into the living room.

"My God, you scared me, Jack. I didn't hear a sound."

"You must have been absorbed in the television. What's on?"

For answer, she turned it off. "Drivel. Are you home for dinner already?" She looked at her watch and then at Jack. "Do you know what time it is?"

"Why don't we eat out tonight?"

"But I've already thawed the meat. I thought you'd grill it and . . ."

"Let's go out."

She looked at him and then slowly smiled. "All right. But she added quickly, "Not at the club."

NINE

HANSON OF THE INDIANA BUREAU OF INVESTIGATION called Andrew on his way in from the airport to tell him that so far the welcome hadn't been overwhelming.

"Weren't you met?"

"Sure, by the sheriff. Don't you have a constabulary in Wyler?"

Andrew smiled at the archaic word. It seemed an appropriate designation for Roland Wilks and his two officers, whose major function in recent years seemed to be to pose an impediment to state police efforts to protect the citizens of the town. In its origin, the main purpose of the town police, over and above making sure

52

John Dillinger didn't try to make an unauthorized withdrawal from one of the banks, was to raise enough money in traffic fines to sustain themselves.

Resistance to the necessary taxes to make the Wyler police a viable force was a sentiment with which he was not wholly unsympathetic. Hoosiers are taxed less than most of their lightly taxed neighbors, yet one often saw bumper stickers declaring that Indiana was the land of taxes. The sales tax and the state income tax ought to be more than enough to provide police protection for the citizens of Wyler, so went the argument, and they did, in the form of the state police. Moreover, the county sheriff had his headquarters in Wyler and his deputies gave the citizenry a sense of security.

"Which deputy picked you up?"

"His says his name is Brownell."

"Eddie Brownell. He'll tell you about our constabulary. You'll find the sheriff easier to work with."

"You going to brief me on what's going on?"

"Better let the sheriff do that."

"Won't I be seeing you? He said you'd be at his office."

"Unofficially, I hope. I'm just a small-town lawyer."

Not long after, the sheriff called.

"Andrew, Hanson of the IBI just arrived in town and I wondered if you had time to drop by while we talked about what you and your nephew found out at the country club yesterday morning."

"You want Gerald to be there too?"

"I don't think that'll be necessary."

Andrew suggested that Abner, Bullock, and McCoy might be invited.

"I already spoke to them, Andrew."

"Chief Wilks going to be there?"

"Andrew, what I had in mind was just a little informal get-together at which we can acquaint Inspector Hanson with what may be involved in Edgar Bissonet's death."

Done teasing, and establishing his own mild reluctance to come, Andrew said he'd be right over.

As it turned out, it was just the three of them, the sheriff, Hanson, and Andrew. Andrew knew the inspector from previous experience and had marveled at his ability to drop into a strange environment and within days see it from the inside out in a way few natives could. More importantly, he had at his disposal the crime labs and technical support of Indianapolis.

"Since you were in on it from the beginning, why don't you lay it out for the inspector, Andrew?"

Andrew complied, welcoming the opportunity to clarify in his own mind what had happened on the golf course that morning. But first he insisted that this was all confidential, just between the three of them. He didn't want to have the Andrew Broom explanation floating around town.

"You in the man's will or what?" Hanson asked, smiling.

Andrew laughed. "He once fired me as his lawyer."

"When was that?" Cleary asked. "I didn't know that."

"We agreed not to publish it in the *Dealer.*"

So what had happened and why had it been thought best to ask Hanson to fly up from Indianapolis?

Yesterday morning, at about eight o'clock, a threesome arrived at the seventh tee to find that an electric golf cart was parked out on the fairway about two hundred yards from the tee. After waiting a bit, when the cart didn't move, they began to holler and shout. That getting no response, they decided to drive through.

As they approached the cart, they had an idea that it belonged to Edgar Bissonet, whose house abuts that fairway and who had a habit of going onto the course at that point, paying little attention to who might be on the tee getting ready to drive.

"Why didn't they stop him?" Hanson asked. "From just driving onto the course, I mean."

"You mean the club? Well, it is a serious thing to bring complaints against members before the committee. It was thought more politic to ask the pro to speak to Edgar."

"Without success?"

"Actually, the pro, Jack Wirth, argued that we ought to give a man Edgar's age more leeway. And we did. Something like that gets you mad at the time, but back in the clubhouse, there are so many things one can blame as having affected one's game, that Edgar's suddenly appearing on the seventh fairway when you were about to drive loomed less large."

The threesome, as they drew nearer, saw something lying beside the cart. This turned out to be Edgar Bissonet, who was lying facedown on the grass. One of the threesome, Bullock, a retired doctor, pronounced Edgar dead. The three then went to the side of the fairway and waved Andrew and his nephew Gerald Rowan through.

"We drove over to the spot where the cart was parked and were amazed to find that there was a dead man lying next to it. I noticed two things that turned out to have significance. The dead man was holding a club, clenched in his hand, and it was a wedge. It can be argued that for Edgar a wedge was as long a club as a driver, but the pro assured me that Edgar made a fetish out of using the correct club even if he never used it correctly."

"What was the second thing?"

"The spikes on his shoes looked as if they had been cleaned. Since the fairway had been cut that morning, and there had been a pretty heavy dew, they should have been full of grass. I had been cleaning my own spikes ever since we got onto the newly mown fairways."

"When was the fairway cut?"

"Around seven. But the most important thing I learned later from the girl who mowed the front nine that morning."

"A girl?"

"Patty Cermac. She actually saw the cart driven onto the fairway—she was by then several fairways along—and she saw someone drop what she thought was an extra bag of clubs."

"Someone drove the dead body out onto the fairway and put it facedown on the ground?"

"That's the way it looks."

"Tell him about Dr. Whelper."

"Whelper!" Hanson cried. "He's always bothering our technical people."

"He is an enthusiast. But he suggested, long before I had talked with Patty, that Edgar had not died where he was found, but had been brought there."

"On what basis?"

"Rigor mortis. Edgar was stiff as stone. Getting the wedge out of his hand was no small matter."

Hanson wanted a clearer understanding of the relation of Edgar's house to the seventh fairway, so Andrew told him of the nine houses that had been built there in recent years, each one individually designed, not a row of development houses.

"We built one for the pro. Edgar's son Matthew has one, several lots away from his father's."

56

"Didn't anyone in the old man's house see anything Or does he live alone?"

"In a way."

Relating Jane Bissonet's tale of her husband's snoring and the need, if the marriage was to survive, of providing him with a soundproof bedroom, Andrew felt uneasy. He pledged the sheriff to perpetual silence on the matter.

"It'll come out, Andrew."

"But not from you?"

The sheriff held up his left hand with the thumb and little finger touching. "Scout's honor."

So Andrew went on to tell of Edgar's soundproof study cum bedroom.

"When I unlocked the door, the place was a mess, Drawers were pulled open, papers scattered about, lamps had been upset, the furniture looked like someone had had a tantrum or as if a brawl had taken place. But, as Mrs. Bissonet pointed out, she would not have heard a thing."

"So what do we have? You're suggesting that in his soundproof room Edgar had a terrible argument with someone and was killed and then his body was taken out to the fairway and deposited there to deflect attention from the quarrel?"

"Is that what I suggested?"

"Who might have it been?"

"Inspector, I locked the study as soon as I saw its condition. It was clear to me that the room had to be carefully examined by experts. Let them answer your question."

"They'll be in with a mobile unit later today."

Andrew decided not to mention that Matthew Bissonet had arrived late for work yesterday, coming in after ten o'clock, and acting more strangely than usual during the day.

Nor did he mention his own return to the study, wearing rubber gloves. He had disturbed nothing, but there was something he had noticed when he glanced into the room about which he wanted to satisfy his curiosity. The monitor of Edgar's computer had glowed greenly in the dark after he switched off the light.

On the screen was a file manager, listing the various directories stored in the computer. Andrew could hardly have asked for a more helpful thing to be on the monitor. There were perhaps a dozen directories indicating the uses Edgar made of the computer, from Lotus 1 2 3 to WordPerfect to Prodigy and CompuServe. Edgar had access to market information and that is what Andrew had expected to find on the screen. But his eye was caught by a directory titled Poetry.

It ran over fifty thousand bytes, which made Andrew even more curious. He activated WordPerfect and then called up the directory named Poetry.

The poems were in various forms: sonnets, poems composed of quatrains with alternately rhyming lines, abab, abba, aabb, and then repeating the scheme, ending with a heroic couplet. There were sestinas, there was blank verse, there was one canzone. Andrew's first reaction had been that Edgar had made up an anthology of poems he particularly liked. But he began to doubt this. All the poems were love poems. They had a similar theme. And a woman's name, Elena, was mentioned in nearly all of them.

Was it possible that this was Edgar's own poetry, written to someone other than Jane? The image of an old man seated at a computer composing love poems to a woman who, as the poems themselves suggested, was younger than Edgar, induced awe in Andrew. He realized that he had not known Edgar Bissonet well at all, but could we know anyone well enough to discern their deepest secrets? In any case, those poems had amazed Andrew.

He found a blank disk, made a copy of the directory's files, and took it with him, leaving the rest to the IBI. He wondered if they would notice the directory named Poetry.

TEN

FOSTER HAD TAKEN A PARTICULAR LIKING TO REBECCA Prell from the time he hired her.

"I promise not to call you a cub reporter," he'd said to her. She had lank black hair, a pale complexion, and lashes that starred out all around her big pale blue eyes, and she was thin as a rail. She was the cutest thing he had seen since he didn't know when.

"That's good, because I'm a White Sox fan."

She wasn't kidding either. She went up to South Bend for the preseason press party for the single A club that was part of the White Sox organization and later when he got some complementary tickets he offered them to her.

"You got someone to go with you?"

The thin lips closed over her large white teeth and her brow wrinkled. "Is that a condition of taking them?"

The upshot was that he went with her. He had never seen a game in South Bend and expected it to be like watching Legion ball, and it was a very pleasant surprise. The stadium made him feel he was at a real game, the home team got six runs ahead and it should have been over, but the Rockford team began to shell the pitcher and the manager waited too long and before the inning was over South Bend was two runs down. But it still wasn't over. With two outs in the bottom of the ninth, the pitcher Rockford had sent in to save the victory walked two men in succession and then, as if to prove he knew where the plate was, served up a chest-high fastball that was hit over the fence.

Foster wrote an editorial about it, the kind of love letter to baseball nonsports writers are prone to write from time to time.

"You make it sound like you invented the game," he was told in the Roundball.

"Foster, some of us have been going up to South Bend for games for years."

"This here's about *baseball*, Willie. We all know the kind of games you play in South Bend."

He hadn't gotten that kind of response to an editorial for years.

What he hadn't said was that a good part of the enjoyment of the experience had been seeing the game with Rebecca Prell. He introduced her to the Roundball too.

"Better be careful though, the place is crawling with good-looking men."

"It's been a long long time since any of them crawled," she said later.

He felt protective toward her because, after all, you bring a woman that young—she was right out of Ball State—into a strange town, living on her own, you want to make sure nothing happens to her.

"Don't you worry about her," Susannah has said.

"I'm not worried about her."

"You're not her daddy. Anyway, she just looks fragile and in need of protection. She's smart and hard as nails. You made a good choice."

Foster came to think that much of Rebecca's effectiveness as an interviewer lay in the fact that everyone wanted to be nice to her, help her out, get her started. He was reminded at the moment of what she had said of Edgar Bissonet when she interviewed him, or at least tried to interview him, for a piece on senior citizens of Wyler.

"Every time I asked him a question, she would answer."

"His wife?"

"Is his wife about thirteen years old?"

"Let me put it this way. You could interview his wife for your article on seniors."

"This girl isn't much older than I am. She's his secretary, or something."

"I didn't know he had a secretary. He's retired."

"I thought she was a daughter, or granddaughter, I guess, but when she was there the second time, I asked. He called her his secretary."

She didn't put it in the article, for obvious reasons, but it reminded her of something she had noticed doing a paper in college. Her examples were Trollope and Henry James and Hemingway. The theme of the paper was the susceptibility of aging authors to very young women, an attraction that a Trollope or a James never quite acknowledged for what it was.

"They never laid a glove on the girl," Rebecca put it. "But Hemingway was knocked out in the usual way."

Foster had read *Across the River and into the Trees,* but what she said made him go back and read it again. There was a real counterpart in Hemingway's life to the Italian countess.

"I hate to tell you this, but what you're talking about is a cliché. There's no fool like an old fool."

She had a theory about that too. All the really good writing was about a cliché. Of course, the writer didn't say that. He made it fresh and new so that if you did think of the cliché you'd see why it was one.

"You're comparing Edgar to these famous authors?"

"They're just my point of reference."

"Don't old ladies do similar things?"

"Of course. Edith Wharton was my female example."

It was no surprise to learn that she dreamed of seeing Rebecca Prell on the spine of a novel. She had gone into journalism the way people used to—this was before Foster's time, of course—as an apprenticeship. The idea was to become a writer, not to spend the rest of your life interviewing old geezers like Edgar who were making fools of themselves over young women.

Rebecca didn't mention the girl in her piece. Edgar himself got only a glancing mention, but her remarks about the secretary stayed with Foster. He thought of asking his girl to have lunch or whatever with Matthew Bissonet's girl and see if she could get her talking—it turned out Edgar had kept her with him when Matthew took over, and she wasn't as young as Rebecca had thought, but she was young—and then he realized that would probably start a rumor. So he just kept an eye and ear open and found that it was one of those "intense but essentially harmless" relationships Rebecca had spoken so knowledgeably about.

Writing about Edgar's death required almost as much finesse as the fact of his secretary had. Foster was aware that Inspector Hanson was working with the obvious hypothesis that someone had killed Edgar and then put his body out on the golf course. He had learned of the messed-up study, which Hanson's mobile unit had subjected to a thorough going-over, pulling the mobile unit into the Bissonet driveway and then easing it over the lawn and parking it level with the patio. For convenience. Of course, Foster talked with Andrew Broom.

"You suppose whoever did it left his fingerprints around?"

Andrew said he didn't know. He did know that fingerprints they couldn't account for had shown up on the golf cart and club.

"They shouldn't have any trouble accounting for those in the study," Foster said.

"How so?"

"Well, I suppose the family's will be found. Jane's . . ." He said it as if the list would be a long one.

"Uh-uh. That was what he actually called his sanctum sanctorum. Jane said she considered the study off-limits."

"A room in her own house?"

"You heard about the snoring?"

"Tell me about it."

"Only if you promise to get it from someone else as well before you use it."

"Matthew?"

"No, no. Ask Cleary."

There was no way he wasn't going to mention that, once Andrew told him. How many men have been wakened by their wives now and again and told to roll over and stop snoring? But this was incredible.

"Marcel Proust," Rebecca said, when he told her.

"I'll have to pass on that one."

She told him about the French author and his corklined room. He was amazed about the amount of lore she had on authors.

When speaking to Andrew of getting fingerprints from Edgar's soundproof study, Foster said, casually, "And of course his secretary's prints will be there."

Andrew looked at him, waiting for him to say more, and it was clear he hadn't known about the girl.

"I'm sure Jane can tell you about her."

"You tell me, Fred."

He told him what he knew, not attributing it to Rebecca, but borrowing on what she had told him.

"I'm sure it's just one of the intense but harmless relationships that so often spring up between elderly men and young girls."

"You make it sound like something to look forward to."

"I'll tell you one thing you can look forward to. Defending the person accused of killing Edgar Bissonet."

"Are you hiring me?"

"Ho ho. But they'll come to you, Andrew. Of course they will. And you won't be able to turn them down."

"They?"

"The Bissonets."

"The Bissonets! Jane Bissonet wouldn't hurt a fly."

"You know who I mean."

It was, Foster supposed, a lawyer's way not to speculate in such matters, but it was becoming plain as the freckles on Rebecca Prell's nose that Matthew Bissonet would be investigated in the matter of his father's death. And given the way things had been going for him, he would probably stand trial as well.

"You may be right."

"The next time I'm accused of a crime, I know I'll come to you."

"Let's hope I'm free."

Quarles was even more closemouthed than Andrew. Fortunately, there were the police, always

64

willing to jabber away, even Inspector Hanson.

"Well, we need someone on the scene, don't we? Someone whose presence there occasioned no surprise if he was seen. The dog who didn't bark, and all that." His pivot tooth pivoted rather dramatically, giving him a slightly malignant look when he smiled. He was trusting Foster to know that Matthew Bissonet was a near neighbor and presumably the sight of him out and about at that hour would not have caught the notice of anyone.

"And of course there is an eyewitness."

"Have you talked with the mower?"

"We are proceeding at all deliberate speed, Mr. Foster."

An autopsy had been done with the doctor from the mobile unit assisting and plans for the funeral had been made. Foster asked Rebecca Prell to write a sensitive and tasteful piece on the grief of the survivors of Edgar Bissonet.

"Lots of glop?"

"Lots of glop."

Her thin little face became incandescent when she smiled.

"Do you suppose I should mention how inconsolable his secretary is."

"I wonder how she is doing?"

"I'll take that as an assignment."

ELEVEN

WHEN ANDREW ASKED HER TO MARRY HIM, AFTER THE death of Dorothy, his first wife, Susannah had reminded him that she was a Catholic.

"I didn't know that."

65

"You did too."

"Won't they let you marry me?"

"Of course *they* will."

"I'll join up, if I have to."

"You don't and you won't."

Andrew was whatever Methodists become when they stop going to church. He said he did most of his praying on the golf course, and Susannah had thought that was beautiful until she realized he was talking about praying his putts went into the hole.

"Don't be irreverent."

"I'm not. God's a golfer, you know."

"An-drew."

"He has to be. Remember that picture of the earth from outer space? It looked exactly like a golf ball."

Andrew continued to pray on the golf course, though he came to St. Luke's from time to time with her, and to her surprise was an old friend of Father Foley.

"We offer reduced fees for the clergy," Andrew explained.

Edgar Bissonet was Catholic and Jane had converted when they married, threatening a rift in the Spencer family, but it had been patched over when the staunchly Episcopalian Spencers considered that, in the wake of Vatican II, the ecumenical council of the early 1960s, it was only a matter of time before the Romans stopped being so pharisaical about Henry VIII and his six wives.

"You have a long way to go, you see," she said to Andrew when they were discussing these matters, getting ready to go to the funeral mass.

"You're the last." He took her in his arms. "I've learned my lesson."

She tried to squirm free; she had been about to put on her dress and she felt suddenly vulnerable to his ardor.

66

"Not before church," she said in a whisper.

"Well, certainly not during."

Andrew had not attended the wake the night before. Susannah was happy to see all the Bissonets and Spencers there, feeling the muted sadness the death of someone as old as Edgar brings, and profiting from the occasion's unifying effect. Many of the Spencers stayed on for the rosary, as many as the Bissonets, among whom the faith was less strong in the second and third generations.

Many early twentieth-century immigrants had adopted a condescending attitude toward Catholics, as if they were new arrivals. But the Bissonets went far back in the history of the country, one branch migrating north from New Orleans when the famous purchase was made, another branch coming out of Bardstown, Kentucky, where Edgar's great-grandparents had been married by Father Badin, the first priest ordained in the United States.

"He owned the land on which Notre Dame was built," Edgar often pointed out. And of course the founders of Notre Dame had come from France to Vincennes and then northward to South Bend.

It was said of Edgar that in his version the country had been founded by the Catholics.

"Out here they came before the country."

This fierce loyalty had not been passed on intact to his descendants. For that matter, he himself had been increasingly grumpy about the changes introduced after the council. Latin gave way to the vernacular, but Edgar remembered when they had been urged to stop using French in public devotions because it hurt the feelings of the Irish.

"Mrs. Broom?" a voice had said at Susannah's elbow at the wake and she turned to look into the tear-reddened eyes of Elena Maria.

"Yes."

"We've never met, but I wanted to say hello."

Andrew had told her of the poetry stored in Edgar's computer and consequently Susannah looked at the girl with special interest.

"Would you like to sit? If I don't get off my feet I'm going to faint."

The Evans funeral home was reassuringly phony, the viewing room and lobby furnished like a residence. Susannah led Elena to a little divan under a round mirror with a rococo frame.

"Oh, that feels good," she said when she sat. To her surprise, Elena was dabbing at her eyes, from which real tears were flowing, all the more noticeable because Susannah had noticed no crying among the relatives of the deceased.

"I'm sorry," the young woman said, biting her lip. "He was so good to me and it seems that whenever someone is good to me they die."

"I'm sure that can't be true."

"But it seems to be."

"You worked for Mr. Bissonet, didn't you?"

"Oh, it was fun, not work. He was writing his autobiography, and I helped him, or tried to. He really preferred to do everything himself. I never knew anyone who was so enthusiastic about the computer."

"His autobiography! How wonderful. I hadn't heard."

"Oh, it will all come out now. He wanted to keep it a secret, in case it didn't interest a publisher."

"He was that serious about it?"

She smiled sadly. "Most of the time. Some days he would declare he was going to destroy it all. I was afraid he would, after all that work, so I made backup copies because I knew, if he did do something foolish, he would regret it and be glad I had saved him from his folly."

"Was it a full-time job?"

"Is six hours a day a full-time job? He paid me as though it was, benefits and everything. He said he didn't want the government after him. Since golfing season began, I came only in the afternoon."

"Then you weren't there the other morning?"

Her eyes narrowed. "I wish I had been. Maybe I could have stopped it."

"I suppose you've been questioned about all this?"

"Will I be questioned?"

Susannah did not wish to upset the girl, a short, rounded, snugly type, whose tears seemed just what one would have expected from her. She ran a hand through her thick mane of hair and then shook it into place. It would be unfair to say that she aged as Susannah talked with her, but she no longer seemed the girl she had at first. And of course any woman who had inspired the poetry Andrew had found, samples of which he had read her, induced a kind of awe.

Andrew expressed approval later when Susannah told him of Elena's making her own copies of Edgar's autobiography.

"It's what I would want you to do."

"Are you writing your autobiography?"

"At my age?"

They went off to church in Andrew's car, despite its lack of funereal aspect. He was reaching an age when such sporty cars would have to be given up, but she didn't want to tell him. Perhaps Gerald would joke about it and Andrew would see the wisdom of confining himself to such vehicles as his olive green Porsche.

The funeral mass is no longer the requiem mass of

yore, but out of deference to Edgar's sentiments, Father Foley wore black and the choir chipped in with Latin, including the lugubrious *Dies Irae.* Edgar, Susannah was sure, would have loved it. Even she felt an aesthetic thrill at this reminder of how it once had been.

The homily, alas, was Father Foley at his worst. He went on about what a wonderful man Edgar had been, a good and loyal husband, a stalwart father, blessed to live to see the second and third generations of his family. Beside her, Andrew stirred and she knew he was itching to comment on this portrait of the saintly Edgar Bissonet.

"At least he didn't claim he was a golfer," Andrew said, when they joined the cortege of cars that would go the cemetery.

But of course what Susannah had been thinking was of the strange arrangement that had permitted the Bissonet marriage to continue, a confidence from Jane that had provided her and Andrew with no end of marveling commentary. As for his children, had Father Foley not heard of the falling out between Edgar and Matthew? As for the second and third generations, Father Foley must have been seeing some of them for the first time.

But most intriguing of all was the lovely young secretary and that cache of love poems stored on Edgar's computer, which had been clearly inspired by Elena.

They went to the club from the cemetery, the Bissonets offering brunch to the mourners, and it was there that Susannah, looking about for Elena, heard at her elbow, "Mrs. Broom?"

She turned, expecting to see Elena, but this was a pale Modigliani-like girl, with a timid smile and a very pretty lime green dress.

"I'm Rebecca Prell, from the *Dealer.*"

Susannah stepped back in flattering amazement. "Of course I've seen your byline. Tell me you aren't old enough to be a reporter."

"Indeed I am."

"And you went to college?"

"Four long years."

"Well, this is a day of mourning. I feel that I've aged a decade."

"I saw you talking with Elena at the wake last night."

"Were you there?"

"I left when the praying started. Of course I wasn't interviewing anyone."

"Is this an interview?"

What a lovely smile she had. The waif became a very attractive woman with that smile. "You looked as if you were interviewing Elena last night. I'm surprised that Mrs. Bissonet put up with it."

"Put up with what?"

"Her husband locked up in a soundproof room with someone as clingy and pretty as that."

Across the room, Elena, wearing a black full-skirted frock with pale gray polka dots and a matching billed cap from the back of which her hair emerged in all its glory, was listening attentively to one of the Spencer nephews of Edgar and Jane. The nephew was clearly enthralled. Most men would be. Why would she have allowed herself to be so attached to an old man that she almost alone wept at his wake?

"Another conquest?" Rebecca Prell asked.

"Meow."

Again that radiant but brief smile. "I guess I am a little jealous of her. Did you ever dream of being the girl other girls just hated? I did. It never happened."

"Is she the girl we're all supposed to hate?"

71

"We girls."

Susannah wondered if she were being chided for suggesting she and Rebecca were of the same age.

When Andrew joined them Susannah thought Rebecca was doing her all to charm him, and succeeding. Maybe Rebecca would realize her ambition yet.

TWELVE

CECIL QUARLES MADE SURE THAT JUDGE MINTZ'S clerk, Louise Schwartz, sat in when he went to lay it out for the judge. You couldn't blame a man for being deaf but you could blame him for not getting a hearing aid and barking at people he couldn't hear as if there was something wrong with their mouths instead of his ears.

"I'll sit in, of course," Louise said, "but he has bought a hearing aid."

"I don't believe it."

"Oh, it doesn't work, but you can't say he hasn't admitted he's been a lip-reader for years."

It turned out to be a gadget placed in the center of the conference table which magnified and transmitted in a wireless way what was said to the headphones Mintz was wearing. Quarles could hardly wait to tell them about this at the Roundball Lounge. It was even funnier because, as Louise said, the thing didn't work. Mintz spent a lot of time ignoring the speaker and fiddling with some adjuster on the earphones as he frowned at the tabletop. It was a hell of a way to get an indictment of Matthew Bissonet.

"His father just died," Mintz said, as if Quarles were kicking a man when he was down.

"I am informed by medical experts that his death was not natural."

"Someone killed him?"

"Someone caused his death."

"What the hell kind of distinction is that? Do you mean they didn't mean to do it?"

Quarles was trying to split the difference between the evidence they had that someone had driven the dead Edgar out to the fairway and left him and the cart there, and Whelper's repetition of his notion that asphyxiation rather than the heart was the primary cause of death.

"I thought he had a heart attack."

"An infarction, yes. There's reason to think it was brought on by asphyxiation."

"Caused by what?"

"That would have to be determined."

The medic working for Hanson thought that the asphyxiation symptoms were compatible with death by infarction, that is, were part of it, not something distinct or that had happened before.

"Not that asphyxiation can be ruled out. But why rule it in unless there is supporting evidence of some kind? He wasn't choked to death or anything like that."

It was the part about not ruling it out that led Quarles to keep that avenue open in the indictment he was seeking.

"Fooling around with a dead body, now, you might want to prosecute someone for that." Mintz leaned toward the contraption on the table as he spoke.

"I am assuming that the person who caused his death removed the body in order to create the impression of natural death."

Mintz was frowning again and fiddling with the dial on his headset. Louise fixed Quarles with her eyes, a

73

shared unexpressed laugh. She was getting this down and in any case Quarles was making the argument to her. Mintz would be guided by Louise, as he usually was.

So he more or less ignored Mintz and laid out for Louise his reasons for seeking an indictment of Matthew Bissonet in the death of his father.

"Can the girl who does the mowing identify Matthew as the one who drove the cart onto the fairway?"

"At the distance from which she saw it, she's unsure."

"There can't be many men as tall as Matthew."

"She only saw him while he was at the wheel of the cart."

"She never saw the body deposited on the ground?"

"I'm not sure."

"Cecil, have you thought what a defense lawyer is going to do to your case?"

Quarles was closing in on the stronger stuff. Matthew's prints had been found all over his father's study.

"A room to which no one but his secretary was admitted? He kept it locked when he was in there as well as when he wasn't. Not only Matthew's prints, but the room was a shambles."

Mintz perked up, obviously fascinated by the thought of a soundproof room in which a man could lock himself up, shutting off the world. Perhaps it sounded a lot like not having even a defective hearing aid.

"How'd Matthew get into a locked room?"

"There was a key on top of the doorframe."

"Were Matthew's prints found on the golf cart?"

"No."

"No? How do you account for that?"

"I don't. But the police investigation continues. If

Matthew is convicted of killing his father, it will become a lesser matter that he carted the body onto the golf course."

"And what's his motive supposed to be?"

He could sense that Louise, whose unexpressed skepticism had been palpable, was with him from this point on. Edgar's youthful companion was clearly news to her. He explained that Elena had at first been reluctant to answer any questions.

"She seemed genuinely shaken by Edgar's death. She should have been. He brought her over from the brokerage office when he turned that over to the son, and it was a matter of complaint among the other employees that she was treated with fawning favoritism by Edgar. They were glad to see her go. Her job at the house is difficult to understand. She said she helped Edgar write his autobiography and did odds and ends."

"You think something was going on?" Louise, wearing a funny little smile, sat forward.

"Speak louder," Mintz roared.

Quarles was about to pull the alleged magnifier closer but Mintz told him not to touch it.

"It's delicate, very delicate. It'll work pretty good for a while and then . . ." He shook his head, but then he glared at Quarles. "Try to speak more distinctly. And louder."

If it was this bad in a conference room, what would it be like in court? Louise's answer to that, during a coffee break, was that Mintz pretended to hear but relied on the transcript. She got notes to him to prevent any serious problem while he was on the bench.

"He ought to retire, Louise."

"Hey, he's my job."

They reconvened with Louise asking again whether

the prosecutor had reason to believe that there was some romantic attachment between the old man and his secretary.

"Matthew Bissonet thought so. He threatened Elena, accusing her of alienating his father from his family, and seemed to suggest she was trying to pressure him to rewrite his will."

"She is the source for this information about a threat?"

"Matthew said similar things to employees in his office."

"How did he threaten her, apart from the implicit charge of actionable behavior?"

"He threatened her physically."

"Any witnesses?"

"Only Edgar, I'm afraid. But remarks at the office suggested that he was disposed to have recourse to violence. One day he began throwing books around his office when he came from his parents' home where he had tried unsuccessfully to talk with his father. He was reduced to sending FAXs and E-mail to contact his father."

"E-mail?"

"Edgar was a confirmed computer buff."

"How old was he?"

"Eighty, going on eighty-one."

Quarles knew that Mintz was terrified of computers and had permitted Louise to modernize her operation only after prolonged resistance. Mintz was convinced that the computer would go the way of the hula hoop.

In the end, he rewrote the indictment with Louise's help, got Mintz's signature, and called the sheriff to tell him to arrest Matthew Bissonet.

He would have felt more triumphant if he hadn't

thought of the sheriff explaining to Matthew that he had the right to call an attorney. Why did he have this irrational certainty that Andrew Broom would accept the task of defending Matthew?

THIRTEEN

THROUGHOUT THE FUNERAL, JANE BISSONET HAD moved with trancelike dignity, accepting the condolences of others, manifesting her own grief in an unostentatious but no less heartfelt manner, and seemed to have become almost posthumous herself, as if with the death of her husband of more than half a century, she too had passed into legendary status.

"I feel that I should have died long ago, Andrew. I mean both of us, Edgar and I. We have gone on and on, leading rather useless lives. Whatever we were meant to accomplish, we have done. I think I can say that to you without the risk of being misunderstood. Yet God saw fit to have us stay on."

"I never thought of a long life as a punishment, Jane."

"That is because you are so biblical, Andrew."

Andrew avoided Susannah's eyes and looked instead at Claire Bissonet. She was more stunned than anything. Her husband had been accused of killing his father and she was here with her mother-in-law to ask Andrew to defend him.

"He couldn't have done it," Jane insisted. "Like all of us at some time, he was capable of wishing another's death, but he would have been incapable of bringing it about."

"I am acquainted with much of the case against him, I think." Andrew noticed that Claire made no similar protestation of her husband's innocence, but in her

77

present state, that was perhaps understandable. "Of course I will represent Matthew. I'll go see him at once. There can be no bail in a case like this, so the best we can hope for is a speedy trial and acquittal."

There was a little gasp from Claire, and Jane, turning to her, took her daughter-in-law's hand. Looking back at Andrew, she said, "You have no idea how reassuring it is to us to hear you say that."

He hoped it would be possible to deliver on the promise implicit in his remark. Everything he now knew pointed to Matthew. The one thing Matthew had going for him was what his mother had said. Andrew did not believe Matthew was capable of killing his father or very likely anyone else. Why did that seem almost a fault in the man? He told Jane, and Claire, that he would be relying on their help in this matter.

"As between me and you, both of you, as between Matthew and me, there can be now no secrets. You must treat me as you would a part of your own mind, with that kind of frankness and with the same confidence that what you say will go no further. Anything, and I mean anything, that may seem to strengthen the case against him, you must tell me, as well as the things that will assure a jury of his innocence."

He rose, anxious to talk to Matthew while the shock of arrest and a cell were still weighing on him and it would be easier to squeeze everything from him relevant to this serious charge he faced. Claire rose and allowed Susannah to take her arm, but Jane remained seated.

"What is the word? Parricide? Could there be anything more dreadful than to kill the one who brought you into this world? My son, whatever his differences from his father, could not have done that."

Then she too rose and Gerald gave her his arm. She

put hers through it, then clasped Gerald's wrist with her other hand, and they went out of his office like an exit on stage.

Andrew went to the window and allowed himself a moment before leaving—giving Susannah and Gerald time to get the Bissonet ladies on their way. The town that lay below him, almost obscured by the great cedars and maples and oaks that lined its streets, had been the scene of many Bissonet and Spencer triumphs over the years. There had been black sheep, of course. One lad lit out for the territory rather than fight in the War Between the States. No principle was involved, just an unwillingness to risk his life. He made and lost a fortune in silver, made another fortune as a farmer, and ended his life as a Franciscan friar after his wife died, perhaps the only Spencer before Jane to go over to Rome. The Bissonet black sheep were less colorful and commanded less admiration from subsequent generations. One had fought a duel in New Orleans over the favors of a Creole girl. His challenger fired and missed but he had shot, and shot accurately. His victory was short. Another shot rang out, from the pistol of the Creole girl, and Amadée Bissonet fell dead. Compared to what Matthew was accused of now, those predecessors of his had been guilty of mere peccadilloes.

"I was glad to hear acquittal is so certain," Gerald said behind him.

Andrew turned. "I always enter a fight expecting to win."

"If I had to argue either side, I would find it easier to argue the prosecution's case."

"I hope you don't offer your services to Quarles."

"What? Join the losing side when you and I are pushing for a speedy trial and acquittal of our client?"

79

"Good boy."

"You're going to talk to Matthew. What should I do?"

"Come with me. I want your advice and counsel."

Andrew realized he meant it. His nephew was what he had discerned him to be a few years ago, fresh out of law school, on the verge of embarking on what would no doubt have been a lucrative and successful career in Chicago. Gerald could have become a consummate specialist in a few years and spent the rest of his professional life doing over and over what he had proved he could do. Andrew had managed to convince his nephew of the boredom of a life he had not yet begun to live. To be a mother, Chesterton said, is to be a generalist, while man, the breadwinner, spends his life on a few things. The successful lawyer in Wyler, unlike his urban specialist counterpart, had to be a mother, and Gerald was occupying the role ever more surely.

"You make me feel that lactation is beginning," Gerald said, when told this before they set out to the county jail and their client.

"Change deodorants."

"I'll have to think about that."

They were arm in arm when they came out of Andrew's office and Susannah turned to look at them. She smiled in approval. "Broom and Rowan."

"And in that order," Andrew said.

In that order they went down the hall, into the elevator, and descended to the basement where they took Andrew's established shortcut to the courthouse. As they emerged from the garage ramp, Fred Foster confronted them.

"You've agreed to represent Matthew Bissonet," the editor said.

"Have I? I haven't read tonight's paper yet."

80

"Will you read that when you do?"

"I had better."

Foster slapped Andrew's arm. "I think you're making a huge mistake, Andrew, but I admire your loyalty."

"Loyalty to whom?"

Foster hesitated, as if embarrassed to say it aloud, then decided not to. Perhaps he would have, if Gerald hadn't been there.

"You know."

"Foster, I think it is your way with words that keeps me a loyal reader of the *Dealer*. Such depth, such insight, such . . ."

Shamed into explanation, Foster said he knew Andrew was doing it for the Bissonets and Spencers and what they had meant for this town.

"Then God pity my client. No, Foster, I am moved by a very simple objective, to fend off attacks on my client's innocence. And to preserve my professional reputation."

"To say nothing of the fee."

"To say nothing of the fee."

"I'm glad it's you and not Frank," Foster called after them as they went up the street.

"What sort of fee will you ask for this, Andrew?"

"That depends on how good a case Quarles is able to build."

Matthew Bissonet was still wearing street clothes when he was brought into the consultation room. He seemed startled to see Andrew, as if he had not been told why he was being taken from his cell. He took Andrew's hand as if it were a life preserver just come within reach.

"Andrew," he breathed huskily. "Gerald."

"Your wife and mother have asked me to represent you. I am here to ask if you want me to."

"I was sure you would, Andrew. You will, won't you?"

"I'll take that as a yes."

"I know my father treated you badly."

"No worse than I treated him. It was tit for tat when he took another lawyer. I had found him too conservative a financial manager and wanted a more adventurous broker."

"My father always fancied himself a swashbuckler of finance."

"Well, he buckled more than he swashed in my estimation, but I suppose in the end he did better by proceeding as he did."

"There was no method to it. He just did things. When I asked him why, he couldn't explain it. It's what I've tried to do, introduce method, rationality, into transactions. It's what the biggest firms do too. Their computers are set automatically to buy or sell when certain points are reached."

It is not unusual for one who finds himself suddenly ripped from his daily routine and put in a cell to want to speak of that ordinary routine when at last he gets a chance to speak into a sympathetic ear. Andrew let Matthew talk on for a time before bringing the visit to its point.

"You are accused of killing your father, Matthew."

"That's nonsense."

"The IBI has been here for some days, they have collected a good deal of data, enough to provide Quarles with a sufficiency to convince Judge Mintz that you should be made to stand trial."

"I didn't kill my father."

Two denials spoken in a way Andrew found convincing. His promise of acquittal had not been based on the firm

82

belief that Matthew was innocent, but now he began to believe that Jane was right and Matthew had not done this dreadful thing, whether or not he was capable of it.

"How am I supposed to have killed him?"

Andrew smiled. "That is the Achilles' heel of the prosecution case, unless something has come up that I am unaware of. The indictment says that you brought about the death of your father by causing him to have the heart attack he was always in danger of having. Knowing that, you brought it about."

"How? By saying boo? I said a lot more than boo to my father without any effect."

"Tell me about that."

"About what?"

"Your differences with your father."

Matthew sat back. "They were just the usual things."

"Differences about the brokerage firm, before he retired?"

"Yes, Yes. As I said, I wanted to introduce method. The odd thing was my father was far more enthused with computers and access to data banks than I am. You would have thought that would have led him to see what I was suggesting as attractive. Andrew, I have come to think that people at home with electronics are dreamers, not practical men at all. They live by hunch and instinct, not logic. They have at their disposal the logic machine dreamed of since Lull and Pascal and Leibniz yet they are intuitionists." His large hands moved as he spoke and the long fingers seemed to dance in air.

"I can see that would lead to arguments."

"There were arguments. I suppose my employees can be made to remember them and it will look bad for me."

"Elena Maria was an employee, wasn't she?"

Matthew was transformed by the question, his

expression grew wild. "No. She worked for my father."

"I understand she continued to work for him, at the house."

Matthew fell back in the chair and lifted his face to study the ceiling as if the starry heavens themselves were visible there. His body grew limp.

"So you know of her."

"Yes."

"I don't know why I'm surprised. What has she said about me?"

"What was her relationship to your father, Matthew?"

He sat forward in sudden anger, then fell back again, as if deciding there were battles no longer worth fighting.

"I don't know. The man was eighty years old, what could it have been? But memories die slowly, I guess, and apparently there is some perverse pleasure to be derived from playing the swain when you are toothless, half blind, and racked with arthritis. When I first suggested to him that there was something unusual about his protective attitude toward her, he blew up. That was seven years ago. She had been with us less than a year then, yet her welfare and comfort were all he seemed concerned about. He fawned over her as he did over none of his children or grandchildren. Do you know what he said when I told him that?"

Andrew waited, knowing this was something Matthew could not keep to himself if he wanted.

"He said, 'she is more to me than a child or grandchild.' Now, what in hell is that supposed to mean? At his age. I told him I was going to fire her. He said no, I'm firing you."

What that turned out to mean was that Edgar retired and Elena went with him to be his secretary at home.

Gerald asked Matthew what the girl's interest could possibly have been, and once more Matthew threw himself forward.

"What a 'girl' like that always wants. Oh, I suppose there is just the sheer enjoyment of having that kind of power over a man. But I know he altered his will."

"How do you now that?"

"A clerk at Frank McGough's told one of my nieces. Just offhandedly. You can imagine what an impact that had in the family."

"So this was all well known in the family."

Matthew gave it some thought. "Put it this way. I was not alone in wondering what she might induce him to do. She was the picture of innocence when I accused her of working on a weak old man. I had just read about Groucho Marx. It's not uncommon."

"What did your mother think?"

"She's a saint who would dismiss everything I've just said as so much nonsense. But then she has developed theories about what inheriting money does to people, none of them good."

"Did she think your father had changed his will?"

"I don't know. It wouldn't have affected her own money anyway. You must know something of their financial arrangements, Andrew."

He knew that it had been a point of honor on Edgar's part that no money should come to him from the Spencers as a result of his marrying Jane. So they had sequestered what she had, an amount which was added to by the deaths of aunts and uncles through the years, and which was in the hands of the bank trust department out of which Edgar himself had emerged.

"You realize you have just laid out the probable basis for the prosecution case."

"Explain that to me."

"You had shown concern for a number of years over your father's relations with Elena and you had recently accused her of seeking to influence your father in the rewriting of his will. Unable to persuade her or him, you finally in a rage killed him."

Matthew nodded. "How?"

"You caused him to have a heart attack."

"How?"

Matthew might very well have hit upon the most effective defense against this circumstantial charge.

FOURTEEN

REBECCA PRELL THOUGHT OF HER JOB ON THE *WYLER Dealer* as analogous to Hemingway's on the *Kansas City Star*. It was an apprenticeship. She had washed her mind of all the journalism courses she had taken, courses in which she had been taught to write like an East Coast liberal. Each year at college a new group took over the student paper and for a day or two it bore a different stamp but then subtly it changed and began to read like most newspapers. The editorials were liberal, the menace was always some assault on mindless liberty. In her junior year the daily had risen to the defense of a student who chose to walk about the campus stark naked for half a day before he was bundled up and taken away. The paper argued that he had a constitutional right to make an ass of himself, so to speak, and it was tyranny and oppression to prevent him. The only redeeming thing in the whole campaign was the title of one of the editorials: "Waiting for Godiva."

Rebecca herself had written an ironic piece she called: "Men Were Born Naked and Everywhere They Are in Clothes." It was turned down. The Voltairian slogan was not even recognized behind the twist she had given it. That piece became the first of those she wrote then rewrote again and again, seeking the clearest and most economical and effective way to write what she had to say. She was still perfecting this instrument as she wrote for the *Wyler Dealer.*

A year or two more and she would move on. As soon as she had completed her first book, she would bring this phase of her career to an end. Where she would go next depended in great measure on the fate of her book. She was prepared for it to be turned down. She was not looking for immediate success. She had studied the lives of her literary heroes carefully and knew that, in some deep sense, there is no literary success. Writing was a way of life, not a means to something else.

She lived in a brick apartment building put up in the 1920s. It was not in good repair, the owner lived in Indianapolis, and it was managed, more or less, by a realtor. There were two apartments on each of the two floors, plus the basement one, which had been intended for a live-in maintenance man. It was this basement apartment Rebecca rented, almost against the advice of the realtor, who kept pointing out its defects. All Rebecca could see was its merits. Kitchenette, bath, bedroom, living room. The kitchen appliances came with the apartment; she painted all the walls chalk white, put a mattress on the bedroom floor, and added a lamp that beamed off the walls and made reading in bed a delight. The living room was her library-study. She made bookshelves of fruit crates she picked up at the supermarket and filled them with paperbacks. She had enough experience moving books to avoid buying books she would have to transport. Most of the books that would go with her had come with her.

The essay on the way aging authors were attracted semiromantically to youth had been rewritten since coming to Wyler, but she did not want Mr. Foster any more curious about her ambitions than he already was. She had been resigned to having no one with whom to talk about her writing until just last week when she had met Bruce Hutton at the laundromat. Her expression when he said he worked in the golf shop at the country club was not the noncommittal one she had intended.

"It's just a job," he said defensively.

"You're still in school?"

He had been out for slightly over a year. A business major who, during the senior year interviews, had suddenly realized that he had put his foot on the wrong path.

"What's the right path?"

He looked at her. "I don't know you well enough."

That could have meant anything so she let it alone. He asked what she did for entertainment. He had reddish hair and a mouth like Michelangelo's *David* and seemed in good shape. She asked him what he did for exercise. They ended up playing tennis and afterward went out for a pizza and the day just kept going on until he told her his ambition was to write science fiction.

The only science fiction Rebecca had ever enjoyed was Miller's *A Canticle for Leibowitz,* but at the moment that was forgotten. First she had to find out how serious he was.

"What are you writing now?"

He told her. In great detail. It was something he worked on every day. "Do you know Trollope?" he asked.

"Do I know Trollope! But what's he got to do with science fiction?"

"Not much. He wrote one book that could be called science fiction, a futuristic one, about euthanasia."

"I don't know it."

"*The Fixed Period.* But the reason I mention it is that he wrote every morning for two hours."

Incredibly, she had found a soul mate in Wyler. And it didn't hurt a bit, professionally, that he worked at the country club where the body of Edgar Bissonet had been found.

"Did you know the son who's been charged with the murder?"

"He's not a member."

"Doesn't he live right on the edge of the course, like his father?"

"It's a great location, whether or not you play golf. You've got acres of front lawn that someone else has to mow."

"You ever been to Edgar's?"

"I know where it is."

"I'd like to see it."

"No problem. When would you like to go?"

"Now."

"Now!"

She nodded, then smiled. She was aware of the power of her smile. She was also aware of the curve of his lips, the indentation at their corners, the outward roll of the lower lip, and the noble scallop above the upper lip.

"You know, it'd be kind of fun."

So they went out to the country club and back to the golf shop and then down to where the carts were parked.

"We'll take Jack's. I'll plug it in when we get back so it will be fully charged in the morning."

She sat beside him and then without warning or sound, the cart began to move. It was like magic. They moved out into the darkness of the course, which became less dark as they put the lighted clubhouse behind them. Rebecca tipped back her head and looked at the sky above, brilliant with a million stabs of light against the darkness.

"Isn't this eerie?" she said to Bruce.

"I'm getting an idea for a story."

She could imagine a science fiction story of her own. Their ship had developed mechanical problems and they made an emergency ejection, landing the smaller vehicle safely on this hitherto unknown planet. Fortunately, their mover worked in this atmosphere and now they were making a reconnaissance mission, trying to get a sense of where they had landed. "I wonder if night is perpetual here," the first officer asked. "Would that be possible, sir?" asked the second. Rebecca was imagining a solar system in which one planet, the one they were on, described an orbit relative to another planet, of such a kind that at every moment of its orbit it was eclipsed by the intervening planet.

"See those lights?" Bruce said.

Houses. She was almost sorry their destination was in sight. This silent movement over the landscape, the smell of the night, Bruce beside her, was very pleasant. It occurred to her that she had never hesitated for a moment to head out into the darkness with him. She just knew he was an okay guy.

He slowed the cart and they rolled along what turned out to be the seventh fairway, inspecting the houses that bordered it.

"That's the son's. Matthew's."

The silhouette of a low house, the windows alight but soft because the drapes were pulled. It seemed a house

90

in a state of shock, its master under arrest. But soon Bruce was pointing out Edgar's place, lighted only on the upper floors.

"Can we go in closer?"

"We won't see much more."

"Please."

He turned the cart and pointed it at the house, remarking that the point at which he turned was where Edgar was found. It made it all so real. Bruce brought the cart to a silent stop and they sat there, looking toward the house. Rebecca saw how easily Matthew could get to his father's house from his. And, though from the fairway the houses looked as if they would be visible to one another, she could now see that hedges six feet in height and more divided the properties from one another, giving each its quota of privacy. No wonder the neighbors hadn't noticed anything.

"Okay?" he said.

Suddenly the precedent and analogy she had been groping for hit her. Andrew Wyeth and Helga, the Scandinavian model he had painted and painted, most often in the nude, his representations realistic to a hair. She had been more than a model to him but most importantly of all she had been an obsession. The Helga pictures, when found, had been a sensation, recording the artist's total infatuation and obsession with his model. She herself was aloof in all the pictures, unapproachable, though unhidden and exposed.

"Wyeth," she breathed.

"Becauseth."

She laughed and the spell was broken. On the drive back they talked, having on the outward journey enjoyed the silence.

"Did you really think of a story?"

"I'll show it to you when I've done a draft."

Ahead, the clubhouse shone in the night, a spacecraft to which they were returning.

"Where do you hope to publish?"

He mentioned some magazines and added, "I've already had stories accepted."

"You have?"

"Didn't I tell you? I am very serious about writing."

"And I am very impressed."

It had been a long date and when he brought her to her door, it ended as well as it had begun. He had both hands on the wheel, he thanked her for a great day, and said he'd wait until she got to her door. His face was half in shadow, half not, and his Michelangelo mouth was emphasized. Impulsively, she reached out and ran her fingertip along his lips, feeling the curve and curl and roll and indentations.

"I've been wanting to do that all day."

"That's not how it's done."

He leaned forward and she lifted her face. A nice kiss, lips to lips. She pushed open the door and hopped out.

"Later," she said, and ran to the door. As she pulled the door shut, she saw his car move off, noisily, unlike the golf cart.

FIFTEEN

LISTENING IN WHILE ANDREW INTERVIEWED MATTHEW Bissonet, Gerald became convinced that the prosecution had their best ally in the defendant. A year or two ago he might have balanced this thought with a negative estimate of a small-town prosecutor. But Quarles was the kind of knowledgeable, experienced, competent lawyer Gerald had come to admire.

Law school has the unfortunate effect of creating in students a univocal way of ranking members of the profession. The big corporate lawyers were the first layer, then the Washington lawyers, in and out of government, the ranks sometimes temporarily including the corporate lawyer on loan, then the great advocacy lawyers, perhaps one or two other celebrity levels, and then a precipitous drop to the level where swarmed the vast majority of the nation's attorneys, working in more or less deserved obscurity.

Andrew might have a romantic notion of his hometown and what the practice of law there was. But Gerald was more impressed by his uncle now than he had been when he joined his firm. It would be absurd to say that men like Andrew Broom were common in the town. Andrew could have excelled anywhere in the legal profession, but men like Cecil Quarles could have done extremely well in at least several legal roles. Cecil was no pushover.

After Matthew was taken back to his cell, Andrew turned and looked at Gerald, as if waiting for him to say something. Gerald decided to keep his counsel. Andrew didn't need the handicap of an associate who thought they were going to lose. Andrew clapped his arm.

"He may not be guilty, but he sure looks it."

"You won't put him on the stand, will you?"

"I think so."

They left the consulting room, waved their way past the guards, and skipped the elevator, following the great granite stairway that snaked along the walls of the rotunda, encircling the open metalwork of the shafts up and down which the cages of the elevators moved on greased runners.

"Talking with Matthew," Andrew went on, "I

imagined I was Cecil Quarles trying to pin him down to a direct, clear answer. Think about it."

"You may be right."

"We'll see."

What Andrew wanted Gerald to do was to compile as complete a dossier on the woman he had taken to calling the Señorita as he could—her origins, of course, but also where she lived, what she did when she wasn't inspiring erotic poetry from the computer of an eighty-year-old man, and whether she had a boyfriend her own age, the lot.

"Don't talk to her though. I want to do that, but I want to know as much about her as I can before I go into discovery."

This assignment had the happy implication that it made talking with Louella, the receptionist in Matthew's office, mandatory. But Gerald started with Stan Trumble, who adopted a woeful expression when he met Gerald in the Roundball.

"Thank God Andrew is defending him," he said, sliding into the booth across from Gerald.

"You think he's guilty?"

"I think we're all guilty. I was raised a Calvinist."

"But we're not all guilty of everything, are we?"

"Nice point. It diminishes the depression of universal depravity. You would have made an interesting theologian. Of course to be a Calvinist is to be a theologian. You're saying guilt implies innocence not simply as an alternative lost prelapsarian condition but as a contemporary contrast. Interesting."

"If only I could have put it so briefly."

A wide, closed-mouthed smile. "Touché. Prolixity is also part of the tradition."

"Did Matthew kill his dad?"

94

"Not in my presence."

"Give me whatever might help in his defense."

Trumble developed a portrait of Matthew as a genial, distracted, incompetent Jimmy Stewart type who had failed or the equivalent at everything he did.

"Like Edgar he began in a bank. In Indianapolis. He is still a legend there. They kept him as long as they did because they knew Edgar. The myth is that he was preparing himself to return to Wyler and go in with his father as the eventual inheritor of the brokerage. The result was constant bickering between the two of them, with Matthew, who had never done anything right, instructing Edgar, who hadn't done much wrong, until there was the big blowup that led to Matthew's ascendancy almost as the chance to exhibit how bad he was."

"Well, that sure helps."

"Maybe when I get the truth off my chest I can come up with some helpful lies."

"The big blowup was about Matthew's incompetence?"

The closemouthed smile again, plus one closed eye. "You're leading the witness. No, of course not. You didn't have to have hearing as keen as a dog's to know it was about Elena Maria. She sat in an outer office, wearing silk dresses and spike heels, surrounded by a nimbus of perfume, aiming fingers one at a time at a keyboard, while father and son shouted about her behind closed doors."

"And Edgar took him with her when he went."

"He was deserting a sinking ship. Matthew would have fired Elena if Edgar hadn't provided for her."

"So what was going on?"

"Do you think the private lives of brokers affect their professional performance?" Trumble asked in feigned shock.

"Were they shacking up?"

"It would have been a biblical performance on his part. Medically speaking, he must have died to the flesh long ago. But they say even eunuchs have yearnings which they satisfy in deviant ways."

"Matthew thinks Edgar was being coaxed into changing his will."

"I understood she already was in it."

"Who told you that?"

Trumble looked around as if the rest of the clientele were following their conversation and he needed confirmation that this was an odd question.

"No one *told* me. It was one of those things one heard through the walls during the One Hundred Years War."

"Well, we'll soon know."

"That's right. When is the will going to be made known?"

Gerald passed on that but guessed that if it weren't before the trial it might be an item in it.

A hush fell gradually over the lounge and heads turned to look at the television over the bar. Hi Massey, a local talk-show host whose program was modeled on successful national ones, was jabbering away. He was on the line with a Mrs. Fritz and they were talking about the upcoming trial of Matthew Bissonet for the murder of his father.

"She says she saw the son go over to his father's early that morning," Ted the bartender shouted in response to the question what was going on. Hi was milking it for all it was worth, making faces at the camera, shrugging, having her say it over and over.

"Alice," he said, "at that time of the morning I don't trust my eyes. You know Matthew pretty well?"

"I know him when I see him and I've often seen him go by our place on his way to his father's. He'd leave his yard, go onto the fairway, and pass within sight of our house."

"And you're sure you saw him go over there that morning, at what time did you say?"

"Oh, it couldn't have been much later than six."

"You get up that early?"

"No, but I was up."

Hi ogled the camera. "Better not go into that."

He went into a commercial, the volume on the set was cut, and people turned and went back to what they were doing. Alice Fritz and her husband and family lived on the seventh fairway between the two Bissonet homes.

"One more piece of the puzzle," Trumble said to Gerald, who suggested they get going. He got off at Trumble's floor, asked Louella the receptionist if they could talk later, and got instant agreement.

"I'll call you before I come down."

"You want to talk here?"

Her disappointment suggested he had proposed a Caribbean cruise. There was something very attractive in her petulant disappointment.

"I'll pick you up. How about lunch at the country club?"

Louella looked down at her dress. "In this?"

"They won't let you in without it."

"Oh you."

He took the stairs the rest of the way and asked Susannah if Andrew was in. She put a finger to her lips. "He's thinking."

"I've got something else for him to think about. Have you heard about Alice Fritz calling up the Hi Massey show and saying she saw Matthew go over to his father's at six o'clock in the morning of the day Edgar was found dead?"

97

"Go tell him."

Andrew, in shirtsleeves, cuffs turned up, crossed legs stretched out before him, listened to the news without visible reaction.

"That's nice. I have been pondering another revelation. The statement that Matthew's fingerprints are not on the golf cart was premature and false. They're all over it. I'm trying to think how, in the ordinary course of things, his prints would be all over it."

"He didn't golf."

"Not since he was a kid. He was pretty good. But he gave it up and was only a social member of the club."

"Now, if only Patty the mower could positively identify Matthew as the one who drove the cart onto the fairway."

"You like a challenge, do you?"

"When is Edgar's will likely to be read?"

Andrew said, "If I were Quarles, I would have asked to see it. Of course we will know if it contains more bad news."

Gerald went to his office and tried to fight off the sense that they were engaged in a losing battle. He hadn't cared for Matthew, who seemed to him to be a whiner, a loser, and out of control. If Andrew lost going to bat for that guy it would be doubly ironic. Had Matthew expressed any gratitude or relief that he was being represented by Andrew Broom?

Gerald called Louella at eleven-thirty and said he'd be down. He hadn't burdened Andrew with Trumble's conversation. In the mood of the office, another load of negativity was not what was needed. Trumble answered Louella's phone.

"She went home to change," he said, his voice rippling with comment. "Here is where you should pick her up."

Forty-five minutes later, Gerald escorted Louella into the dining room of the club. She was wearing a yellow dress that seemed pasted on her: it had a deep vee neck and stopped many inches above the knee. Green heels helped put all of her into proportion.

"Oh, let's sit by the window."

Gerald had intended they sit out of the way so they could talk but soon they were placed like a floral display in front of the massive window overlooking the course and being asked if they wanted anything from the bar. Louella wanted an old-fashioned.

"Beer," said Gerald, to move the barman away from her side. He seemed fascinated by her décolletage.

For twenty minutes, Gerald told himself that this had been a mistake, he should have invited her to a come as you are lunch at Burger King. She smiled relentlessly, looked vacantly around as if inviting attention, and getting it, until Gerald doubted there would be any talk worth having. It was nonetheless pleasant to sit with so fair a flower and feel as invisible as the fellow who throws the ballerina around.

"Elena loved coming here," she said, leaning over the table.

His instinct was to lean forward too, prudence suggested leaning back, but what she had said gave the nod to instinct.

"Did she?"

"Well, she certainly went on about it. Being seen with him seemed to be the extent of her ambitions."

Louella's eyes grew wider as she said this.

"Then you don't think there was anything . . ."

"I don't think one way or the other," she said primly.

"It seems on the face of it unlikely."

"I suppose." She seemed to doubt it.

"Didn't she have any friends her own age? Male friends."

"Oh heavens yes. But friend, not friends."

"Aha."

"He is very serious. Very." She made a long face and frowned. "And he didn't like her working for Edgar."

"Do you know his name?"

She laughed. "Of course."

"Can you tell me?"

"Isn't that why we're here?" And she pursed her lips and narrowed her eyes. "I am no fool, Gerald Rowan. So I will pay the piper."

She waited, teasing him, and he put his hand on hers, willing to coax her, and smiled his most winning smile. At which point he was distracted by several women who had entered the dining room and come to a halt, waiting to be seated. Still wearing his seductive smile, Gerald found himself looking directly at Julie McGough. She looked at him, she looked at his companion, she looked at him again, coldly, and turned away.

"Is something wrong?"

"No, no. Of course not. Who is he?"

"You look as if you're going to be ill."

"I really don't feel well." He looked at her salmon salad that she had been stirring about as they sat there. "Nearly done?"

"But I haven't told you the name of Elena's very jealous boyfriend."

He looked at her. He could not have smiled if everything depended on it. She became serious.

"Hector," she said. "Hector Sonora."

SIXTEEN

MATTHEW DID NOT WANT TO SEE HIS WIFE. HE HAD settled into his cell like the Prisoner of Zenda and told Claire he might write his autobiography like his father.

"He feels disgraced, Susannah. No matter what happens, the name Bissonet will never again mean what it has meant in Wyler."

"Claire, Andrew has promised that he will be acquitted. He has done nothing wrong."

"Oh, he doesn't mean himself. He means his father. Edgar has made the name Bissonet a laughingstock."

The problematical death of Edgar and the arrest of Matthew had been the talk of the town for a day or two, but life did go on and there were people, the majority actually, who may not have thought of the name Bissonet for days. But Matthew was in the eye of the storm and could scarcely be expected to adopt the carefree indifference of the unaccused.

"In any case, he is prepared to be found guilty."

Susannah grew wary as Claire spoke, fearing that she might now receive a confidence that she would have to conceal from Andrew. Should Claire tell her that her husband had indeed brought on his father's death, Susannah would consider it information received under the seal of the confessional. The last thing a defense lawyer needed was a disinterested statement that his client was guilty. But Claire's interest was all the other way. She was taking her husband's indictment and arrest harder than he was, for all his theatrics as a prisoner.

"I think I know what happened."

"Oh."

"I hesitated about speaking directly to Andrew and thought it would be easier if we talked."

Claire held one hand very tightly in the other and sat rigidly across the table on the Bissonet's patio. Somewhere out on the course, Andrew was playing the game he loved. Susannah felt she was on the verge of the wife's admission that her husband was guilty.

"Knowing what this has been like for us, I hate to put anyone else through the same thing."

"I don't understand."

"Susannah, I think I know who may have done this and then made it look as though it was Matthew who had."

"Tell me."

"Remember, I am not making an accusation and if you think it best, don't even mention it to Andrew. But the more I think of it . . ."

"Claire, who do you think killed your father-in-law?"

Her hands separated for a moment and then she gripped her right hand with her left.

"Do you know who lives two doors up?" Her head indicated where she thought up was.

"Two doors?"

"The Wirths, Jack and Mona. This is not really a very social neighborhood, despite the way we are all nestled in here next to the fairway. The dividing hedges are like blinders on a horse: we look out at the course but never at one another. When you think of the fact that Matthew doesn't even golf, it becomes even less probable."

Claire meant that she and Matthew had become friends with the Wirths, the couples playing bridge together, just getting together on their patios at night.

"We have so little in common that we just enjoyed one another. He is an athlete whereas Matthew is, well,

Matthew. And Mona . . . Do you know her at all?"

How could any member of the country club not know Mona? She was a trim, tanned woman with silvery blond hair who could golf like a dream but had lost interest in it. And acquired an interest in drink. And harmless flirtation.

"Oh yes."

"Matthew fascinated her. I mean what he does, and of course that fascinated him. I'm afraid he became a bit of a bore, going into great detail when she would ask him silly things like what the difference is between a stock and a bond. He asked her to come down to his office and he would show her around. She did, he did."

Far off on the course, a triumphant cry went up as some player made a putt. A blue jay landed on a dogwood tree just off the patio and looked angrily about.

"Matthew mentioned the visit several times and I think he was trying to tell me that he had been surprised by her. She didn't care at all for stocks or bonds."

"She is a terrible flirt."

"I'd known that. I thought it was just her manner. Matthew is so, well, Matthew, he might not have understood the difference between the serious and the not."

"He thought she was serious?"

Claire nodded. Clearly she found all this painful. "Then Jack Wirth came to me."

"He did!"

"Yes. He told me that he thought something was going on between Matthew and Mona and that we, he and I, had to do something about it. Susannah, he was deadly serious. I could see that it wouldn't at all do to laugh it off."

103

"What did you do?"

"I talked to Matthew."

"What did he say?"

"Susannah, it took him a while before he understood what it was Jack Wirth suspected him of. When he did, he wanted to go over and punch him in the nose."

"Good for him."

But Claire had released a hand and it lifted to stop Susannah. "Punch him in the nose for insulting his own wife!"

And then Claire laughed, but it was the kind of laughter that is a first cousin to crying and Susannah sensed how terrible recent events had been for her.

"He didn't punch him in the nose?"

"No, but he told him he ought to have more respect for his wife. If he knew her better, he would realize what she was and what she was not capable of."

"Oh no."

"Oh yes. Jack Wirth took a swing at Matthew and actually hit him. Matthew was astounded. Jack Wirth wanted to know when Matthew became such an expert on his wife."

The friendship had ceased but Jack Wirth's suspicions did not. He called Claire several more times, urging her to keep a close watch on Matthew, as he was on Mona. He said he knew something was going on and when he caught them he was going to kill Matthew with his bare hands.

"Not a very pleasant neighbor to have."

"I would never have dreamed anything like this could happen when we first became friends. Jack always struck me as such an untroubled person, not really grown up, spending his life playing a game, enjoying all day long what members pay large amounts to enjoy from time to time, and he got paid for it. It seemed such a pleasant, shallow existence."

Susannah looked out over the course, at the shades of green revealed and created by sunlight filtering through the trees and by the occasional passage of a cloud. Andrew often spoke of getting away from the real world when he went golfing, but golf was the only world Jack and Mona Wirth knew. Susannah had never imagined the club pro was a jealous husband. Had Claire exaggerated what Jack had said to her? And what implication did she think what he had said might have?

"You don't seriously think that it was Jack Wirth who killed Edgar and wheeled him onto the fairway?"

Her lip trembled. She looked helplessly at Susannah. "What I do know is that it could not have been Matthew. I suppose Andrew would think I'm crazy for even mentioning this."

"He would have thought you were crazy if you hadn't."

SEVENTEEN

WHENEVER CECIL QUARLES CAUGHT HIMSELF whistling while he worked, he bit his tongue and looked sheepishly around to see if anyone had noticed. He had Blake and Konstantin and the summer intern Collins working on the Edgar prosecution, Blake and Konstantin taking depositions, Collins finding precedents for convictions for murders that involved using the victim's health problems as a weapon against him. That was the tack Quarles was taking.

"We need a smoking gun," Blake said more than once, seeming to address Collins, who had finally put

105

away her pinstripe suits and was dressing for the weather and the season.

"No gun is involved."

Konstantine had volunteered to talk to Whelper, who had unexpectedly gained an ally in Wooster, the medico from Indianapolis Hanson had brought up. At first, Wooster doubted that the autopsy had turned up anything but the infarction that had killed Edgar. But further reflection, and study, had led him to agree that it was not impossible that asphyxiation might have contributed to the heart attack that killed him.

Quarles wanted someone else to talk with Whelper and Konstantine said he'd do it, but if it became necessary Quarles himself would sit down with the enthusiastic doctor who occupied the nonexistent post of medical examiner.

Mintz had read over the record of the meeting in which he had issued the indictment and was having second thoughts. Louise told Quarles that the most the judge now saw was someone moving a dead body around without authorization. It was time to play the Whelper card.

For all that, Quarles felt giddy he was so confident in his case. Once he had accepted the fact that the evidence would be almost entirely circumstantial, he saw that the jury must be led from point to point in such a way that it converged on only one possible verdict. No one had actually seen Matthew Bissonet induce a heart attack in his father, but Matthew's fingerprints were everywhere. Alice Fritz, his neighbor, now placed him at the site at the time when death had most likely occurred. His motives were many, but Quarles intended to concentrate on Matthew's fear of the influence of Elena Maria on his father. Underlying it all would be the rapacious greed of the already rich. Blake had interviewed the young woman.

"He was like a father to me," she told him.

"An eighty-year-old man?"

"His heart was young."

"It was also very weak. You give your age as thirty."

"That is my age."

"And Edgar Bissonet was eighty."

"He was like a grandfather to me."

"How long had you known him?"

"Slightly more than seven years."

"Are you mentioned in his will?"

"No."

"How do you know?"

"I don't know. That's what I meant."

"Did he give you gifts?"

"A father could not have been more generous."

"Does the phrase Sugar Daddy mean anything to you?"

"*Azúcar*? What is *toddy*?"

"Forget it."

Blake had the impression that she was like a kid who wasn't playing fair in a guessing game.

"Do you think there was hanky-panky?" Quarles asked.

"Cecil, he was eighty years old."

"Makes you wonder, doesn't it? Remember Charlie Chaplin."

Her Chilean boyfriend Hector was there when Blake continued the deposition and his presence had a chilling effect on the questioning. Hector's hair was ebony, his skin caffè latte, and he wore, visible at his unbuttoned collar, a heavy gold chain about his throat. His teeth beneath the Xavier Cugat mustache were wide and

107

white. ("Cecil," Blake said later, "I've heard of Charlie Chaplin, though I don't know what you meant by your reference, but who in hell is Xavier Cugat?")

"Why are you asking Elena Maria these questions?" Hector Sonora asked.

"She worked for a man named Edgar Bissonet."

Elena Maria put a hand on Hector's arm and assured him in their common language that everything was all right. At least, that seemed to be the message. He lit a cigarette and, though he didn't go away, looked with lofty disdain at his surroundings. Perhaps he didn't understand the questions.

"What is Hector doing in this country?" Quarles asked Elena Maria while Blake was distracting Hector.

"He is an exchange student."

Quarles wondered what we had given in exchange. "He's from Chile?"

"Santiago." She smiled. "It is my city too."

How in the world a girl from Santiago, Chile, ever got involved with an old coot like Edgar in a small Indiana town was a puzzler. Asking about it got the conversation going in circles.

"Why did you come to Wyler?"

"To work for Mr. Bissonet."

"But why did he hire you?"

"To work in his office."

"You saw the Visit Wyler, Indiana, posters in Chile and decided to come?"

"That is a joke, no?"

"Did you know Edgar before you came here?"

"He knew me."

"Ah. And how did that come about?"

She smiled directly into Quarles's face. "He knew my father."

108

When he asked the defendant where she had come from he said he supposed that she had swum the Rio Grande. "She's hardly a rare bird, Cecil. Look around you. Farming would go belly up without all that cheap labor."

"You think Elena Maria is a farmworker?"

Andrew sat in Quarles's talks with Matthew. Cecil was playing this one entirely by the book. He wasn't going to give Andrew a procedural goof to put them all back on square one again.

"Great line of questioning," Andrew said afterward.

"It was stupid expecting Matthew to know anything about the girl."

"She's the key, Cecil. Pursue her trail."

"Just establishing motive."

EIGHTEEN

"YOUR CLIENT IS GOING TO SWING, ANDREW," HANSON said jovially when they got together for a farewell lunch before the IBI man and his cohorts headed back to Indianapolis.

"For what? No crime has been committed."

"Is that your defense?"

"We have a dead man whose body was moved after he died. Dying is no crime, moving dead bodies around is, but that's not what my client is accused of."

"I thought it was part of the package."

"That's the prosecution's big mistake."

"So who killed the old guy?"

"For purposes of this trial, I'm going to claim he died a natural death."

"You'll get negative medical testimony on that."

"Which I can counter with other medical testimony."

Hanson puffed on his cigar and watched his exhaled smoke as if it carried a message. "When I came up here I thought what you think. Where's the crime? Now I'm convinced he was half asphyxiated and that brought on the heart attack."

"What's half asphyxiation?"

"A botched job maybe."

"Any marks on the body indicating he was strangled?"

"Cutting off a person's air is the easiest thing in the world," Hanson mused. "Oh, you may have to be stronger than your victim, and it takes a while, but it's easy. Take a fish out of water and watch him flop around for a few minutes and then he's dead. Drowned in air. Cut off a person's oxygen supply and you get the same result. There's no mark on the fish."

"That's all speculation."

"Is it? The old guy slept in that soundproof study. A pillow is the simplest instrument for this kind of murder, provided one is handy. Plastic sacks are nice."

"Lots of them lying around the study?"

"Yes."

"Come on."

"On the shelf in the closet are stacks of the old guy's shirts. They come from the laundry in individual plastic sacks."

"Any missing?"

"Yes."

This was bad. Hanson said that the plastic bag for the shirt Edgar was wearing was accounted for. It was in the wastepaper basket in his john. But one of the shirts on the shelf was not in its bag. "Very likely that was the weapon."

110

"What happened to it?"

"By the time we checked the trash receptacles on the course, they had been changed. Quarles needn't produce the actual bag, need he?"

"I'm sure the jury would like to see it."

"Oh, he can show them one just like it."

"But that's not quite the same thing. Why not just stay with saying Edgar was strangled?"

"Because he died of a heart attack."

"By natural causes."

"Natural causes can be unnaturally activated."

"Do you think a jury is going to find Matthew guilty of murder on the basis of such a conjectural story?"

The answer, Andrew knew, was probably yes. The resentment factor in jury decisions is hard to calculate, but every lawyer knows it is there. Put a wealthy playboy in the dock and the prosecutor is going to make every possible allusion to the accused's style of life. Matthew Bissonet was no playboy but it would be easy to describe his life as one of sybaritic comfort to jurors who would rather be doing something else anyway.

Despite this depressing turn, Andrew went on to what had been his chief purpose in inviting Hanson to lunch.

"I've been looking over your report on the contents of the hard drive of Edgar's computer. You listed all the directories, all the files?"

"All of them."

"So I don't have to worry about Cecil Quarles springing a computer file in which Edgar expresses his fear and terror of his son and expects him to make an effort to kill him?"

Hanson chuckled. "Everything stored in the computer is on that list. You can take a look at it yourself, can't you?"

"I intend to. And there are no diskettes or storage tapes or removable drives or anything like that on which other files might be kept that didn't make it onto your list."

"You are a trusting soul, aren't you?"

"Just thorough. Is your answer no?"

"My answer is no."

Hanson in Andrew's experience was a straight shooter, and he was not inclined to doubt his word, but he had to pursue this line.

"The prosecutor couldn't have removed any files before your people examined the computer?"

"Maybe he could have, but he didn't. Thanks to your precaution in locking the door of the soundproof study, nobody could have." Smoke trailed from the corners of his mouth. "Unless they had a key."

"There were only two. One was found in Edgar's pocket, the other I gave you."

"His secretary?"

"She had no key. Nor did his wife. The one above the door was there for her use, in an emergency."

"I have a feeling you are after something in particular, Andrew."

"Just the truth, Hanson. Just the truth."

And he moved them away from the subject, before Hanson might think to ask Andrew if he himself had checked out the computer before Hanson's team did.

There were two things missing from the hard drive, the autobiography Edgar had been writing, and his love poems to Elena. Andrew had made copies of the poems, Elena had made copies of the autobiography.

When Andrew had copied the poems, his intention had been simply to have them so that he could peruse them at his leisure. He had not destroyed the original file and he had been sure that the poems would figure in Quarles's argument that the relationship between Elena and Edgar had been such that Matthew would understandably have been troubled, even enraged, by it. But the poems had disappeared. Along with the autobiography.

The following day Elena Maria came to his office for her pretrial deposition.

"You could have brought a lawyer with you."

She beamed at Andrew and threw a special smile at Gerald, who had welcomed her. "But I have no lawyer. Gerald said you simply wanted to talk."

Gerald! "True. But we will be talking about things you may be called to testify on in court. Sometimes it is advisable to have a lawyer to consult before you answer."

"Then Gerald can be my lawyer!" She didn't quite clap her hands at this inspiration.

Andrew explained that Gerald was representing the accused. This meeting would seek to find out facts, truths, which could be used to show that Matthew was innocent of his father's death.

"Oh, he didn't kill him."

"You're sure of that?"

"I will say so in court."

"What makes you so sure?"

"His father said he would never do such a thing."

"You discussed that with Edgar?"

"Several times. He would say, 'Matthew would kill me if he knew this or that,' and then he would laugh and say, 'No, Matthew wouldn't hurt a fly.' "

"What would you be discussing when Matthew's killing him came up?"

She rolled out her ripe red lower lip and tipped her

113

head in thought. "Different things. Things he put in his autobiography."

"I understand you made a copy of that."

"He said he would erase it. After all that work. And it was so interesting."

"I'm sure." Andrew tried to imagine an interesting account of the life Edgar had lived, that is, interesting to the lively young lady before him, and failed. "Would you take a look at this listing of the things stored on Edgar's computer, the one in his study?"

Gerald helped get the printouts laid out before her. She went down the list, using her painted nail as a guide, nodding as she went. "Yes, yes, yes." She looked up. "I know all these well." She went back to the record, Gerald turned the page, she continued and then was done. "Those are all Edgar's files, yes."

"Can you find the autobiography files there?"

"They're missing."

"Missing in what sense?"

"They're not on the list."

"Isn't that surprising?"

"The poems are missing too."

"The poems to Elena Maria?"

"They are beautiful, beautiful," she sighed.

"And now they are gone."

"Oh no, no no. The originals still exist. I typed from them onto the computer."

"You have the originals?"

"Of course."

"What form are the originals in?"

"I don't understand."

"Are they printouts, typed, handwritten?"

"Oh, written. Elegantly written, You can see at once that they are love poems."

"Does the autobiography exist in written form as well?"

"Oh no. He would dictate and I would enter what he said directly into the computer."

"So the backup copies you made are now the only existing version of Edgar's autobiography."

"Yes, that's true."

"I hope you have them in a safe place."

"Oh yes. I sent them home to Chile."

It thus appeared that two items that might have figured in the case against Matthew were *hors de combat*. Those poems would have been difficult to interpret as the products of a Platonic relationship. As for the autobiography, Andrew had the notion that, by dictating the story of his life to his inamorata, Edgar would have been powerfully tempted to engage in folly similar to that of composing verse to Elena. Far be it from him to suppress evidence. No one could say that he had. He had erased neither the poems nor the autobiography from the computer. And apparently the originals of the poems were in existence.

The question arose, who had done it?

"Have you been asked for your key to Edgar Bissonet's study?"

"I have no key to the study."

"I should have thought he would want you to have one."

"Why? I worked for him and if he were not there there was no reason for me to go in."

"You've noticed that neither the autobiography nor the poems to Elena appear on the official record of the contents of Edgar's computer. They're absent from the list because they're absent from the computer. Someone erased them."

"He threatened to do that," Elena said sadly.

"So you think Edgar removed those materials from the computer?"

"Who else could have done so?"

Later, bringing Matthew up to date and trying to impress upon him the seriousness of his position, Andrew asked how Matthew's fingerprints came to be all over the soundproof study.

"I was looking for proof of his damned foolishness with ChaCha."

"You mean Elena?"

"Conchita Banana."

Even now, Matthew could not speak of the girl without anger, sarcasm, contempt.

"When did you make this search?"

"That morning."

"The morning your father died?"

"Yes."

"How did you get into the study?"

"My father let me in."

"What time was this?"

"Some ungodly hour. I hadn't slept a wink. The night before, my father and I had talked and it had ended on an infuriating note. As I had several times before, I asked him if he had changed his will. He said my questioning had made him think of doing it. He had dictated some notes on the matter. Dictated. That means he talked it over with Paprika herself. I told him what I thought of him. I left in a great huff, tossed and turned all night, and came back in the morning determined to see those notes."

"Did you find them?"

"I tore the place apart looking for them. He was

116

already dressed in one of those absurd outfits he wore while golfing. He sat there grinning as I searched. When he had said notes, I thought of something written on paper. But of course my father was a total devotee of the computer. I found what I was looking for there."

"Notes on changing the will?"

"Worse. The old fool had written poems to her, dozens of them, awful sentimental mush. And he was writing an autobiography, one that began in the present and progressed backward into the past."

"You read it?"

"Enough to see what it was. It was written in the form of a long letter to Elena and he was promising her to go back to the time they had met, she was to be patient, he would recall everything."

"Then what?"

"I called him more names and left."

"He was still alive?"

"Of course he was still alive."

"All dressed up to play golf."

"He even had his spiked shoes on."

"Had you looked in your father's closet?"

"I looked everywhere."

"Is that where he kept his shirts?"

"Yes. I swept them from the shelf and they sailed across the floor."

"So they would have to go back to the laundry."

"No no. They come from the laundry in plastic bags."

Matthew mentioned this with no hesitation.

"I am not proud of the way I acted. The thought that an old man could make such a fool of himself simply enraged me. I lost control."

Andrew had felt that things looked bad when Hanson mentioned the shirt which was missing its plastic

117

wrapper. Now Matthew had blithely made the circumstantial case against himself far stronger.

"Did you tell anyone about the poems and autobiography on the computer?"

Matthew stared at Andrew. "My wife, of course. I was still roaring when I got home. Why do you come back to those poems and his life story?"

"Because someone erased them from the computer's hard drive."

"I wish I had done that."

"But you didn't."

"No."

NINETEEN

FRED FOSTER THOUGHT THE *DEALER* OUGHT TO DO ITS own investigating into the death of Edgar Bissonet, but it simply didn't have the staff necessary to duplicate or compete with the official investigation. Rebecca suggested a kind of impressionistic inquiry into the relationship between Edgar and Elena Maria.

"It couldn't be done without running the risk of a suit for libel."

"I don't mean an exposé. It would be a reflection on things already in the public domain."

"Comparing Edgar to those writers you mentioned."

"I thought of another parallel. Andrew Wyeth."

She told him about Helga and he followed with rapt attention.

"I don't think Edgar had her posing in the nude."

Rebecca told him that wasn't the point. She didn't want to do a sensational piece. This would be an effort to understand, placing the known relationship between

Edgar and the girl into a pattern exemplified by many others.

"Not just writers and artists. Businessmen reach an age when they dump their wives and marry someone half their age."

He was wary of the idea. The best she could do was to get a go-ahead to rough out what she had in mind so he could decide definitively on the basis of that.

Trumble in Matthew Bissonet's office proved to be a flowing font of information. He and Rebecca sat in his office where computers blinked and an electronic tape ran and faxes rolled in, activities that prompted him to do things seemingly with only half his mind involved.

"You're pretty good at this, aren't you?"

"Yes."

"How much money does it take to open an account?"

"Is that an idle question?"

"I don't have much."

"Rebecca, let me have what you are prepared to risk, and I will make you rich."

"Can you promise that, responsibly?"

"I can tell you how to get rich with virtually no risk at all. You are, what? Twenty-five?"

"Twenty-three!"

"Even better. If you opened a savings account and added to it regularly until you are thirty, and then just forgot about it, compound interest would make you wealthy by the time you retire."

"So why should I invest?"

"It's quicker. Of course you could do both."

"Do you follow your own advice?"

"Absolutely."

"Does everyone who works here?"

He raised his brows. "There are improvident ones, alas."

"How about Elena, was she in the market?"

"For what?" He burst out laughing. "Sorry. No, she didn't have a dime's worth of stock."

"She was one of the improvident ones?"

"*Au contraire,* or its Chilean equivalent. Not only did she have the old gentleman eating out of her hand, she had a *caballero* as well."

Thus it was that Rebecca heard about Hector Sonora, the *caballero* she eventually tracked down. He was perfectly willing to talk. Hector was studying at Ball State on a Fulbright fellowship and came to see Elena as often as possible. He had loved her in Chile but social mores made it impossible for him to be alone with her there.

"Her mother is worse than any duenna. An eagle eye." He pulled down the skin under one eye. "Very protective. This is a powerful aphrodisiac. The tempting but forbidden?"

"I understand."

They were in the student union at Ball State, sipping Coke, and talking. He understood her to be gathering materials for a piece on Fulbright exchange students from Latin America. Rebecca mentioned that she knew a Chilean girl in Wyler. He was amazed. Elena Maria was his true love.

"Her employer recently died."

"She will never go back to Chile."

"You will?"

"Of course. She feels at home here, but then she has been here longer than I. I am sick of home."

"Homesick?"

"But for her I will stay. I mean, come back. I must

return to Chile after this semester. An exchange student cannot just stay."

This provided the theme of her next talk with Elena.

"I met Hector," Rebecca said.

"He is nice, no?"

"You're a lucky girl."

"My mother does not approve of him."

"Why?"

"He has no culture or breeding." She smiled. "But she disapproves of all young men."

"I'm surprised she let you come to the States at all."

"It was to get me away from Hector."

"And now he is here."

"Maybe my mother is right about him."

"Would your mother have approved of Edgar?"

"Oh yes, certainly. That is entirely different."

"How?"

Elena studied Rebecca with half-closed eyes. "You are twenty, twenty-one?"

"More or less."

"Young women in this country know little of love. All they hear about is sex, sex, sex, but nothing of love and romance, of wanting what you cannot have, the lure of the forbidden, giving in as much out of desperation as desire."

"Wow."

"You understand."

"In your version too it seems to end up as sex, sex, sex."

Elena sighed. "You are all Puritans still."

Such volatile shifts, accompanied by a truly amazing range of facial expressions and body language, the eyes ever asparkle with the suggestion of complicity between

121

speaker and hearer, would charm, Rebecca supposed, most men, and apparently she had worked her magic on Edgar Bissonet. Rebecca was forming and re-forming the type of young woman who figured in such April/December liaisons. Perhaps there wasn't a type.

In any case, the theory she brought to her interviews with Elena wasn't much help and no theory emerged from talking with her. And so she came to Jane Spencer Bissonet.

"There has been altogether too much publicity already," she said, and her cool gray eyes rejected Rebecca's admittedly phony suggestion that Mrs. Bissonet should have a chance to put the family's point of view before the public.

"It will get worse once the trial begins."

"The trial." She put her hand to her face and for the first time Rebecca realized she was a very old woman. There seemed little flesh in the hand, the back of which was spotted, the veins prominent. How could the widow of Edgar Bissonet be other than ancient? But there is beauty in age, and this woman had it—a general serenity along with the sad conviction that all things go wrong in the end.

"Could we talk? I'd give anything just to get off my feet."

Rebecca's comments on the house, when she was asked in, had led to a tour and once they had taken the little escalator down to the level looking out at the golf course, they went onto the patio and sat. When she looked out at the course, Rebecca imagined herself and Bruce there in the dark, parked in the golf cart, staring at this house.

"This is where it happened, isn't it?"

"Just out there." She nodded in the direction Rebecca had been looking.

"Were you up yet?"

"Oh yes." She smiled. Were those her own teeth? "One is always tired when old but sleep is rare and fitful. Edgar was already out on the course so I came down to make his bed and clean up his study. That room was his apartment, you see."

"You saw him on the course?"

"Yes. It's odd to think that I was tidying up his bathroom, hanging up his pajamas, making his bed, and he was already gone."

"I wonder what time that would have been."

"Early, quite early."

"What time did his secretary come?"

"She didn't come at all, there was no point."

"I mean usually?"

Jane laughed. "Oh, she kept what we used to call banker's hours. We would have tea before she went down to Edgar."

"You and she had tea together?"

"Yes. Our little ritual."

"You must have liked her."

"She wouldn't permit anything else. Have you met her?"

"We've talked, yes."

"I wonder what she told you."

"Nothing much."

"I'm not surprised. Would you like tea?"

"I couldn't put you to the bother."

"I mean to ask you to go for it. There is iced tea in the refrigerator."

Rebecca went for it and brought down pitcher and glasses, lemon and sugar, on a tray, following instructions.

123

"Edgar and I often sat here in the evenings. He hated iced tea. Isn't it peaceful here?"

"Yes. It seems sad that he died here."

The old woman looked at her with an odd smile. "But that was the point of this house. We came here to die."

TWENTY

WHEN REBECCA PRELL CAME BY THE OFFICE Susannah appeared in Gerald's doorway.

"A young lady to see you," she said musically.

Gerald was half on his feet, afraid that Louella would replace Susannah in the doorway, so that when he saw the reporter, he half shouted a relieved greeting. While he got her seated, he was aware of Susannah the matchmaker trying to catch his eye from the hallway but he was practiced in ignoring the ongoing effort to deflect his interests from Julie McGough.

"I can't believe we haven't met," he said.

"You must not be newsworthy."

"What does that take? Killing someone or being killed, public indecency, speeding . . ."

"You are defending Matthew Bissonet."

"That's newsworthy."

"The prosecutor seems pretty sure he's going to get a guilty verdict."

"His case does seem strong."

"But not strong enough?"

"Matthew Bissonet will be declared not guilty."

"Wow."

"I quote the senior member of the firm, Andrew Broom."

"A legend in his own time. Or at least in his own town."

"Do I detect a note of irreverence?"

"I suppose neither you nor the prosecutor knows how it will come out?"

"Well, we're both willing to go through with at least the formality of a trial."

"I've talked with Mrs. Bissonet, the widow."

"A wonderful woman."

She talked about her interview and Gerald wondered if he had ever heard before that Jane had kept the soundproof apartment tidy for her husband. Later, after Andrew had come in and he passed her along to him ("Don't leave without coming back," he said to her. "So far I've done all the talking." "That's why I want you to come back."). Gerald busied himself making a corrected breakdown of that fatal morning.

The factors to be chronologically ordered were these:

1. The discovery of the body of Edgar lying beside his golf cart on the seventh fairway by the threesome of Abner, Bullock, and McCoy.
2. The arrival of himself and Andrew on the seventh tee.
3. Patty mowing the seventh fairway and waving to Edgar on his patio.
4. Patty mowing the fifth fairway and seeing Edgar's cart being driven onto the seventh fairway.
5. Matthew's coming to see his father, shouting, tearing up the study.
6. Jane, seeing the cart on the fairway, tidying up Edgar's study.

The temporal order of these events seemed to be: 5, 3, 6, 4, 1, 2. About to seek greater precision by assigning clock times, Gerald was struck by the incompatibility of

5 and 6. Jane could not have tidied up the study after Matthew had been there, because Edgar was in his apartment at the time. And Jane had not tidied up the apartment, since it had been found in chaotic condition when Andrew unlocked the door. A reconciliation of these facts was possible if one posited a third event: 5, then 6, but also:

7. The arrival of someone else who created the chaos Andrew found when he opened the door.

That someone else could have entered the study was clear from the fact that someone *had* entered it and erased from the computer the poetry and autobiography files. This had occurred after Andrew's own surreptitious entry into the soundproof study. But who other than a member of the family would select the poetry and autobiography files for deletion?

Gerald summarized all this in a memo for Andrew and when Rebecca peeked in again asked if she was ready for lunch.

"Lunch?"

"I'd love to."

She loved the idea until he suggested going to the country club, saying she'd rather stay in town.

"I've already been out there this morning," she said.

"You make it sound a hundred miles away."

It occurred to him that running the risk of having Julie see him with yet another lovely young lady in the dining room of the club was madness. It would be wiser to cede to Rebecca's wishes.

"There is a sordid little place just downstairs called the Roundball Lounge. Greasy sandwiches, hard liquor, beer, a high level of noise and excitement, very popular."

She said she knew the place, but they went anyway. He got her stashed in the booth, a beer before her, sandwiches ordered, then excused himself, wanting to call Andrew. Eschewing the phone in the lounge, he went into the lobby, where he ran into Julie.

"Gerald," she cried. "I just took the chance I'd find you."

She was wearing her all-is-forgiven smile; proximity to her once more filled him with the certainty that this was the woman he loved and must eventually marry.

"Well, here I am."

"Lunch?" How promissory the monosyllable became as it issued from her mouth, which retained its shape after pronouncing the word.

"I can't."

"Just that? I can't?"

"It's this darned Edgar Bissonet defense. I have to talk to Andrew."

"You just came out of the lounge."

"The need hit me as soon as I sat down."

"The need?"

"To talk to Andrew."

"Well," she said, drawing herself up in a way that made him gasp. "Perhaps another time."

She went on into the lounge. Gerald fought the panic he felt, continued to the pay phone, and called the number of the lounge. Minutes went by, the phone ringing and ringing, but of course this was the midday rush.

"Yeah?"

"Willie?"

"Yeah."

"This is Gerald Rowan. Listen very carefully. The girl I came in with? Go tell her to come out into the lobby immediately."

127

"That's the message?"

"I'm out here."

"And you're telephoning me to . . ." The phone slammed down.

Gerald waited, wondering if Willie would or would not do as asked. He was thinking of crawling through the lounge to the booth and whispering to Rebecca, when she appeared in the door of the lounge. He waved her to him. She frowned, then came reluctantly toward him.

"We can't eat in there."

"But we already ordered."

The door of the lounge spun and out came Julie. She was almost upon them when she noticed them. She stopped, her lips parted, she looked at Rebecca and then again at Gerald. Her expression was murderous. Gerald's reaction caused Rebecca to turn. Her eyes must have met Julie's. Then Julie went rapidly to the street door and outside.

"Who was that?"

"A client."

"She seemed angry."

"Did she? She's often that way. Shall we reclaim our booth?"

TWENTY-ONE

WHEN, AT THE AGE OF SEVENTEEN, STAN TRUMBLE had resolved to become a millionaire before he was twenty-five, he had thought of wealth as purifying, elevating, a sign of virtue. To call this Calvinism would amount to theological libel, no doubt, and in any case his resolution proved stronger than his allegiance to the

128

faith of his fathers. He had last trembled to the message of a Dutch Reformed sermon when he was nineteen whereas, at twenty-eight, not yet a millionaire, he was in willing thrall to Mammon.

The assumptions of his resolution had been modified, of course. The seventeen-year-old Trumble who had made his solemn vow was proximately prompted by the awe induced in him by the godlike members of the country club, whose cars he was parking one fateful autumn evening. He had been hired just for the occasion—some special seasonal bash, he could not even remember what it was—and with several other groundlings waited offstage under the porte cochere of the club where sleek expensive cars slid to a stop and disgorged their passengers. Doors were flung open, a trim ankle or black shoe thrust out, and then with a rush of talk, laughter, smoke, and perfume, they disappeared inside. Trumble would get behind the wheel of the still-purring car and ease it down the drive and into the parking lot, where he would leave the numbered card in the window and hurry back to deposit the key in a box bearing the matching number.

That had been his sole contact with the country club and this contributed to the mythic power of the event. No peasant had been readier to tug his forelock in the presence of his betters, but equally no peasant had been more resolved to eventually become his better.

When to a counselor at college he had replied in a jocular fashion to the question about his aim in life, "I want to be rich," the equally jocular reply was, "Well, there's no specific course for that." It was the best advice he ever got. What if he had majored in economics, or, dear God, in business administration, or some other practical subject meant to prepare him for the real world? The world of money was as ethereal as poetry, as unmappable as Mars—the great amassers of wealth had all been dreamers. Let clerks and aides and assistants and future vice presidents of this or that take those practical subjects, he would become a generalist and keep himself on the alert for the big chance.

On his shelves were books by and about his heroes. Monks once had meditated on the lives of saints for guidance in their own quest for sanctity. Stan Trumble's shelf was lined with the lives of Ford, Hughes, Gates, Fuller, Hefner.

He did join a stock club as an undergraduate, stayed with it for the several weeks it took to grasp the point of the process, then appropriated seven hundred dollars of the club's funds—a housemate was treasurer—and within months of frantic, feverish, and exhilarating buys and sells, had more than enough to restore the missing money and save his housemate from expulsion, if only from the club, and was well on his way, he imagined, to his first million. He felt as libertines do when they first discover sex. He neglected everything else in order to play the market. He became thin and pale but he was deliriously happy. He had several hundred thousand dollars when a margin call came at an inopportune time and wiped him out.

It was a salutary lesson, playing the role that the acquisition of a minor venereal disease might play in alerting a potential libertine to the dark side of sex. The elements of the lesson were: sin boldly but remember that the devil like a roaring lion goeth about seeking whom he might devour. A wave of thefts swept his student residence—he himself claimed to have lost his very food money—and he was once again in the market. He had never looked back since.

130

On graduation, he realized that he knew as much about the market as anyone, surely a good deal more than business majors or economists. He was, at the time, four hundred thousand to the good and he had transferred half of that money into tax-free bonds. Although Trumble finally absolved himself of the debt, his housemates, who had unknowingly financed him, weren't so lucky. "Ought implies can," as he had learned in a philosophy course, and vice versa too: you cannot be obliged to do something you cannot do at all. There was no way he could have slipped all those diverse sums back to his housemates.

The obvious arena for his talents was Wall Street. Only a few years earlier, to do what he intended to do would have dictated such a move. But the computer had changed all that. The story of Microsoft had so captured his imagination that he would have been drawn to the computer even if it had no particular relevance to his ambition. But of course it did. The market was now accessible anywhere, by personal computer. It was thus that he had earned his wings, subscribing to various databases, trading via the computer night and day as he played both the European and the Oriental exchanges. Singapore had been particularly good to him. He might have continued as a freelance but some residual Calvinist caution suggested that he find a job. Where better than back home in Wyler with Edgar Bissonet?

And Matthew too, alas. If there was anyone not cut out for the craps game of investment it was the son of Edgar Bissonet, SOB, as Stan came to think of him. Matthew had gone to Yale and apparently knew nothing. He didn't just know nothing about the thrill and adventure of manipulating money electronically, with wealth as immaterial as little numbers appearing on a monitor;

Matthew had never read Booth Tarkington, after whom one of the main streets of Wyler was named; he had not read William Dean Howells, Willa Cather, or Edward Arlington Robinson. He thought Gödel's Theorem was a plan for underwear. He looked blank when Trumble had cited that marvelous title, "The Vice of Gambling and the Virtue of Insurance." The suggestion of course was that what they were engaged in was gambling. Never explain a joke. Matthew was shocked.

He did, however, prove to be a malleable pupil in the matter of the computer. The bank from which he came to join his father had apparently used abacuses, but Matthew listened and with conversion became a vocal and boring advocate of computerization. He was preaching to the choir, of course, since old Edgar had long since succumbed to Trumble's same pitch. Matthew's knowledge was limited, needless to say, and his scruples got in the way of excellence in the field. When Elena Maria, daughter of an old acquaintance of Edgar's, came aboard, Trumble considered the possibility of an alliance.

She got them in ahead of the privatization curve in Latin America and accounts were showing 17 percent a year. She got Trumble personally into Argentine and Chilean companies and overnight, as it seemed, he was a much wealthier man. Unfortunately, her learning of the investments he was making ostensibly for Edgar jeopardized Trumble's use of the old man's money as a source of ready capital.

"I speak to you in great confidence," Elena said to Trumble.

"Yes."

"There has been a steady and significant loss from Mr. Bissonet's investments."

"Matthew's?"

She shook her head and put her hand on his arm. If he were not quaking at the prospect of imminent exposure, he would have enjoyed this moment live as much as he did in reruns in his memory.

"I think unauthorized sells have been made."

"That's hard to believe."

"You have known Edgar longer than I have."

"True."

"There are reasons why I cannot tell him what his son has been doing."

His son! Trumble put his hand over hers. "You want me to?"

"Would you?"

"It would destroy the firm. Unless . . ."

"Yes?"

He sketched for her an ad hoc plan whereby the two of them would repair the damage Matthew had done while at the same time she would convince Edgar to retire. What did he do at the office that he could not do at home?

"I would miss him so." She seemed sincere. She spoke of loyalty, of love. Clearly she had her limitations as an ally.

"Go with him."

Her dark eyes shone. Thus from the nettle danger he had plucked the flower safety. Apparently. The parting of Bissonet from Bissonet was amicable. Matthew clearly thought he could do better without old Edgar around to hold him back. There was an office party to commemorate the departure of their founder. Edgar took Trumble aside.

"I see that the ravages to my personal portfolio have been repaired."

"Yes, sir." Had Elena told him after all?

"It might be hard to get an indictment in Wyler for electronic theft, particularly when recompense has been made."

Bring charges against his own son? Trumble was readying himself to counsel against this when Edgar continued.

"But if you try such a stunt again, young man, I'll see to it that you spend the rest of your life in prison."

And he moved stiffly away, leaving Trumble to ask himself who was duping whom.

The conviction grew in him that Elena had suspected the truth and ratted on him to the old man. He was as glad to see her go as he was Edgar. But life had been uneasy since. Matthew, on his own, and getting very little help from Trumble, became a nervous wreck, and Trumble, to guard against accusation from Edgar, began to draw on his own funds to cover the stupidities of Matthew. Flush as he was, his assets could never hope to trump the witless way in which Matthew managed clients' accounts. Trumble had found himself facing the very real possibility of being wiped out in an effort to avoid being wiped out by an accusation from Edgar. Something had to give.

He calculated that with a hundred thousand and working just the Tokyo Exchange, he could trade himself back into some semblance of affluence.

"You told Edgar of Matthew's peculations, didn't you?" he said to Elena, in an effort to find out if she were the source of the old man's certainty about his losses.

"Never! His own son? I could not. And you must not either."

If this was not sincerity, Trumble was headed for a Tibetan lamasery.

"He's at it again, Elena."

"No!"

"I can show you."

She waved away the printouts he had brought. They were seated on Edgar's patio. The sun slanted through a maple tree and mottled the lawn and patio. Birds sang. Some ineffable peace and contentment seemed available on those well-tended grounds. A shout of anguish split the air. Trumble looked at Elena.

"A missed putt," she said. "What do you intend to do?"

"What we did before."

"Ah."

"But I need a kitty of a hundred thousand."

"You could borrow it from Edgar."

"Is he here now?"

"No, there." She pointed toward the fairway. A lone figure of a man leaned over the wheel of a golf cart, headed to the left. Other golfers, Trumble had noticed, went in the opposite direction on that hole. He commented on this. "He plays just that one hole. Nine times if he's up to it. Back and forth, back and forth."

"Odd."

"Golf is odd."

Another anguished cry was heard.

"Come into his study with me."

They went across the patio, through a large room to a door which Elena could not open. "I've locked myself out!" She covered her open mouth with both hands. When she removed them, she was smiling.

"Above the doorway," she said. "You can reach it,"

He found the key and handed it to her and they went inside the soundproof room where Edgar dwelled. Eagle's Nest? Fuhrer's Bunker? The latter. Adolf did not die at Berchtesgaden.

135

TWENTY-TWO

STATE OF INDIANA V. MATTHEW BISSONET GOT underway with jury selection and it said something about what lay ahead that Cecil Quarles seemed disposed to settle for any twelve citizens pulled at random off the street, whereas Andrew had long exchanges with members of the venire. Either those who made it would resent what he had put them through or be more responsive to his defense out of a sense of achievement.

Meanwhile, Gerald had come up with what seemed to be an exact chronological sequence of the events of the fateful day.

"I hear Trumble is to be called early on by Quarles," Gerald said.

"I thought you found him helpful."

"Talkative, not helpful. If he says on the stand what he chattered about to me, the jury will wonder how Matthew stayed out of jail so long."

"What is he, jealous?"

"It's hard to say. He likes to run down people he works with. Elena Maria sings his praises, says he is the most brilliant man she ever worked with—except for Edgar, that is. I think he's been ready to break loose from Matthew. Maybe he'll salvage the wreckage."

Quarles's opening statement took five minutes; he spoke in grieved tones, as if the task of asking them to find a son guilty of his father's death weighed heavily upon him. Maybe it did. When it was his turn, Andrew spoke slowly, occasionally consulting a slip of paper as if surprised to find it in his hand.

"Your Honor, ladies and gentlemen, we have come

136

here to waste taxpayers' money in what will certainly be a failed effort to make you believe that this young man, Matthew Bissonet, still in mourning for his father, killed his father, a father who had lovingly raised him, expensively educated him, taken him into his brokerage firm, showed him the ropes, got him settled, and then himself retired to enjoy his golden years with his dear wife, close to Matthew and his family, playing the game he loved, golf. The prosecution has no case. You cannot convict a man of murder when no murder has been committed. You cannot have a murder without a murder weapon. The prosecution has no murder weapon. You cannot have a murder, certainly of the kind imagined here, without a motive. The prosecution has no motive. It is not my task to prove my client's innocence. As he sits there he is as innocent as you or I. But unlike you and I he has been accused of a crime that did not occur, in a manner that cannot be explained, for motives that do not exist. I will try to be as expeditious in my defense as possible, both for your sakes and for the sake of the taxpayers of the State of Indiana."

The impact of this statement was promptly diluted by Mintz, who pointed out that an indictment had been brought according to the procedures of the State of Indiana and the jury could rest assured that this trial was not simply a private whim of the prosecutor.

While Mintz spoke, Andrew busied himself at his table, half rose to look into the audience, and in general did what he could to distract the jury from the judge. But when Quarles continued the response as he rose to call his first witness, Andrew interrupted.

"Your Honor, I am always willing to have the jury enlightened by remarks from the bench, but if the prosecutor wishes to debate our opening statements, I

137

shall be happy to do so, irregular a procedure as that may be."

"Call your first witness," growled Mintz and Quarles called Dr. Bullock, who was duly sworn and identified himself as a retired physician in Wyler.

"You were golfing at the country club on the morning of July 17, Doctor?"

"I'm retired," Bullock said defensively.

Quarles chortled good-humoredly and assured Bullock that he understood perfectly the right of a retired person to golf as often as he might choose to do so. Andrew asked if the prosecutor would restrict the right to the retired. Quarles denied giving any such implication. Mintz growled that he was delighted to see that Mr. Broom intended to keep his promise to save the taxpayers money.

"Will you describe for the jury what you and your golf partners discovered on the seventh fairway of the country club golf course on the morning in question?"

Bullock did so, in prolix detail. He would have been willing to describe each of the six holes leading up to the seventh, but was persuaded by Quarles to concentrate on the hole where the event of interest to these proceedings took place.

"When we found the body of Edgar Bissonet? We saw the cart parked out there when we were on the tee, and we waited although only McCoy had ever driven a ball that far. We couldn't see anyone on the fairway."

Andrew intervened. "Your playing companions reported they could see no one?"

"That's right."

Quarles wanted to know if they could not follow established procedure and he be permitted to interrogate his own witness before the defense cross-examined.

138

"Your Honor, I intervened to see if we do indeed have a witness here. If Dr. Bullock is here to tell us what his companions told him, it might be a wise thing for the prosecutor to call them."

"Dr. Bullock was not called to tell us what he did or did not see from the tee, Your Honor. He is here as a witness to what he, and the others, found when they got out onto the fairway, and he has been selected from the three because he is a medical man."

"Let's get him onto the fairway then."

Bullock's description of the discovery of Edgar's body was vivid and to the point. The golf cart was parked twenty feet from a sand trap and the body lay facedown on the opposite side of the cart.

"And you could see that he was dead?"

"He was dead."

"Where was the golf cart parked relative to the home of the deceased?"

Mintz found this question unusual and asked that it be prepared for and Quarles backed up and asked Bullock where Edgar Bissonet lived. Andrew of course rose.

"Your Honor, is Dr. Bullock now an expert on the location of the residences of all and sundry?"

"Everyone knows where Edgar Bissonet lived, Your Honor."

"I don't," Mintz snapped. "And even if I did it cannot be assumed that the members of the jury do."

Quarles himself undertook to establish the location of Edgar's home and he was happy to let Bullock go, having established that the body of Edgar Bissonet had indeed been found on the country club golf course on the morning of July 17.

"Did you examine the body, Doctor?" Andrew asked

139

after making a tour past the jury box and then returning to a spot before the witness stand.

"No!"

Andrew expressed astonishment. "You say you did *not* examine the body."

"There was no need for that."

"I don't understand."

"I have seen my share of dead bodies, sir."

"I'm sorry to hear that, Doctor. Have you ever declared a patient dead by just looking into the room at him lying on a bed?"

"Rigor mortis had set in!" cried Bullock indignantly.

"Ah, so you tried to move the body?"

"I did not. My God, Andrew, you were there. You saw the grip he had on that sand wedge."

"Counsel for the defense also discovered the body?" Mintz asked. Clearly he hadn't spent a great deal of time preparing for this trial.

In due time, Bullock was let go and Quarles set about seeking to establish the time when death had occurred. There was no way he could avoid bringing Whelper to the stand. The doctor turned self-made criminal medical examiner came eagerly. He was inches less than six feet tall but his stride was that of a giant, giving the impression that he was engaged in cross-country skiing when he walked. He raised his hand as if in salute and the oath was administered. Once seated, Whelper leaned forward, elbows on the edge of the witness stand, ready. Quarles approached the stand slowly, warily.

"Medical examiner," Whelper boomed, when asked to state his profession.

"You are a physician?"

"And surgeon!" Whelper looked as if he would be

140

happy to carve up someone in support of this statement. The jury was taking an interest.

"What in your professional opinion was the time of death?"

"Between six-twenty and six twenty-five of the morning of July 17."

"You can be that precise?"

"Our ability to determine these things has made enormous strides in recent years."

"So Edgar had been dead for hours when Dr. Bullock and his friends—including the defense attorney—came upon his body on the seventh fairway?"

Whelper nodded as if Quarles was doing just fine. "Of course he hadn't died where he was found."

"He hadn't!" said Cecil in mock surprise.

"No sir, he hadn't. He had died elsewhere and been brought to the spot where he was found."

"Is this conjecture?"

"This is science!" But here Whelper was relying as much on what Hanson's team had determined as on any findings of his own.

"And of what did he die, Dr. Whelper?"

"Of two things. The initial verdict was death by infarction and that was true as far as it goes. But I was not satisfied. I continued my investigations and I am happy to say that the team sent here by the IBI agreed with me."

"We'll hear from a representative of that team later, perhaps. What did your further investigations reveal?"

"There were signs of severe oxygen deprivation, asphyxiation. It is my belief that an attempt was made on the deceased's life in the course of which he had a heart attack."

The jury was unaware that Whelper was a figure of

fun to the coroner and to the sheriff and to the chief of police. He spoke with authority and the jury hung on his every word. It was Andrew's task to turn Whelper's testimony to his own advantage.

"Given the amount of time that intervened between the death of Edgar Bissonet and the discovery of his body on the golf course, I suppose we can say that death might have occurred anywhere," Andrew began. "I mean anywhere within say three hours' drive of where the body was found."

"I have proceeded on the assumption that death occurred at his home."

"After which person or persons unknown drove the corpse onto the fairway?"

Quarles intervened to say that he had a witness who would so testify. Andrew said that he was aware of that, having had something to do with discovering the witness in question.

"But, Doctor, if it is established that the body was brought onto the golf course an hour, even an hour and a half, prior to its discovery, there is still unaccounted-for time, giving your estimate of when death occurred."

"I suppose that's so." Whelper said this slowly.

"What earthly reason is there to suppose that it is so?" Quarles cried out and was warned by Mintz.

"Well, it can't be ruled out."

"Score," whispered Gerald, but Andrew was not proud of himself. Whatever he had scored could be taken away by testimony Quarles would no doubt bring. Patty's testimony as to when she had seen the body being driven onto the course would alone remove the hypothesis that Whelper had allowed.

Quarles summoned Patty Cermac then but Mintz said he was going to call it a day.

142

"A day, Your Honor?" Quarles was astonished.

"Normally, we will reconvene in the afternoon, but today we won't."

And Mintz, absolute monarch of his domain, slammed down his gavel and rose, the whole court rising with him.

Over lunch with Susannah and Gerald, Andrew felt the unease of the morning increase. He did not like the way things were going. Patty would be called, Hanson would be called, Alice Fritz, the neighbor, would be called, everything that had been turned up since Edgar's death would converge on the guilt of Matthew Bissonet. The defendant himself had been preoccupied before he was taken back to his jail cell. Was he guilty after all?

Meanwhile, Gerald and Susannah were telling one another that things had gone well in court, that it was a good beginning.

"Where did that opening statement come from, Andrew?" Gerald asked in admiration.

"I wonder what my closing statement will be?"

He could see how depressed they were by this uncharacteristic gloom. He had never lost a serious contest in court, and that record had given him confidence. He had gone into the defense of Matthew Bissonet with a cockiness that invited a reversal. Confidence was one thing, the resolve to give his client the best defense he could, but it was something else to suggest that he could not lose. He could lose. And if he lost and Matthew Bissonet was innocent, that would be loss indeed.

"How will you use the afternoon?"

"I think I'll golf."

Gerald said he couldn't go, doubtless seeing that Andrew wanted to be alone. Andrew took a roundabout way to the country club, calling ahead to have his clubs ready. What was eating at him were those files missing from Edgar's computer. Hanson's printout indicated that he had no idea they were missing, and presumably Cecil Quarles was equally in the dark about them. Those who knew they were missing would have little incentive to make them known. Someone had regarded them as sufficiently important to remove them. Had Edgar suddenly realized his foolish infatuation for Elena and removed the files from his computer? Only if he had risen from the dead.

Imagining that there might be a sudden revelation of the missing files, Andrew asked himself what damage they could do. The poetry established that Matthew had reason to fear the influence of Elena Maria, but that fear could be established on other grounds. Andrew assumed that the autobiography, begun in the present and working backward, written in the form of a letter, would also reveal the old man's unusual relationship with the young woman.

So why should he worry about those missing files? Because they were missing.

From the parking lot, before going in to change, he called the office and asked Susannah to have Gerald try to coax a copy of the autobiography from Elena Maria, asking her to have it sent from Santiago directly to the office.

That removed his unease somewhat and then came the locker room, changing, spending some time on the practice green, being enveloped by the special world of the course, all of which lifted his spirits—at least for now.

When he arrived at the first tee, there was a lull and Jack Wirth waved him off as a singleton.

"Come along, Jack."

"I've got work to do."

"Golf is your work."

Still, he was glad to be by himself. The idea of Jack Wirth being jealous of Matthew Bissonet had been upsetting. The club pro was one of Andrew's best friends, a straight shooter, seemingly untroubled by the passing annoyances that others could not ignore. But there are surprises lurking in everyone, although most of them remain hidden, and we deal with a public personality that may be very far from the real person.

But Jack Wirth too was forgotten when Andrew rode up to his ball. He had driven it to an unusual point in the fairway, deliberately, as a challenge, and it was a question what club to use. He could take a nine iron and bring it in high, toward the back of the green, and let backspin bring it toward the hole. Or he could live dangerously, chip and run it between the two traps guarding this approach to the green. He lived dangerously. The ball landed where he had aimed it but then seemed to lose momentum in the fringe. It made it onto the green nonetheless and then kept on rolling to within a foot of the pin. By now his world was bounded by the game he was playing.

He birdied the first and second holes and on the par three almost holed out his tee shot. Another birdie. The sense grew in him that he was embarked on a historic round, and one that would have no witnesses. It was not that he thought his card would be doubted, but it always meant more when other players witnessed an exceptional round.

He came to the fifth hole three under and determined to get at least a birdie on this par five. He didn't tee up his drive and sent it on a low powerful trajectory to a point on the right-hand side of the fairway. Perfect. He was considering his next shot when the sound of a far-off mower reminded him that this was the hole from which Patty had seen someone drive the body of Edgar onto the golf course. He glanced toward the seventh fairway. It was not yet visible from where he was, but he could see the roofs of the houses built along it. He continued toward his ball, from time to time glancing toward the seventh fairway. He still could see neither the point where Edgar's cart had been parked nor his house. He had reached his ball and still had not reproduced the view that Patty had said she had got of the cart being driven onto the course. This was puzzling.

He turned and headed back toward the tee. There was no one following him so he took his time. He started out from the tee again, asking himself if the height of the mower would account for Patty's being able to see what he couldn't. He spent ten minutes, looping back and forth, and then finally went to his ball. When he addressed it, he concentrated on the shot he was going to make. He was using a driver and he meant to put the ball next to the pin for an eagle possibility. Concentrate on that. Forget for the moment that Patty had lied to him about what she had seen that fateful morning.

TWENTY-THREE

REBECCA WAS IN THE COURTROOM, BUT NOT AS A reporter. Foster himself was covering the trial for the paper. She had not volunteered, as he had thought she would, when he talked to her about the need to be fair and thorough in their coverage of the Matthew Bissonet trial.

"Is the transcript available after each session?"

"Why?"

"Could we get permission to run it every day?"

"I doubt it. A fair summary, giving the highlights, is what our readers expect of us."

That's when she was supposed to say, Mr. Foster, let me do it, let me cover the trial. But she didn't. So why didn't he just assign her to it? Because if he did, more experienced reporters were going to resent it. He had sensed resentment lately, and perhaps it was deserved. Rebecca was an interesting young lady to have around, but chances were she would move on quickly to something else and he would regret jeopardizing the general good feeling on the paper to make her stay with them more interesting. So he announced that he himself would cover the trial, but he worked out a schedule that involved everyone who could have any claim on it as well. After all, attending a trial was like going to a play, and there weren't many journalists who could resist it.

"Could I have press passes?" Rebecca asked.

"Passes?"

"I want to bring a friend."

He gave her two passes if only to see who her friend was. Nice-looking kid he had seen somewhere before, he couldn't remember where.

"The golf shop," Gerald Rowan said when Foster asked if he knew the boy.

"This trial may ruin Andrew's game."

"Do you think Matthew killed his father?"

"It's what those people in the jury box will think."

Foster didn't believe that Matthew had killed his father, but then there were all kinds of indisputable truths he could not imagine. How many married couples could he actually imagine in bed together? Since most

147

of them had children they must sleep together, but it was the kind of thing you had to take on faith. So too Edgar was dead and his body had been carted around in an undignified way, he had quarreled with Matthew, and apparently had a crush on the Chilean girl who worked for him—Foster contested none of these, but he couldn't imagine them. The fact that he couldn't imagine Matthew killing his father meant little, accordingly.

What he kept returning to in his mind was Edgar's strange relationship with his secretary. Half a century at least separated the two, yet Foster had been given to believe that the old man had written sheaves of poetry to her and that they spent the day working on his autobiography, a narrative he had undertaken for the young woman's sake. How obvious the folly of others is. Foster realized that his unease was due to his own intense attachment to Rebecca Prell.

There. He had formulated the thought and recognized its truth. He might not be fifty years older than Rebecca but he was capable of as much foolishness as Edgar Bissonet. Hadn't he felt a twinge of jealousy when he saw Rebecca enter the courtroom with Bruce Hutton from the pro shop?

It seemed to him now that everyone else had long since seen what he had just acknowledged. Had Rebecca herself been trying to tell him this when she kept bringing up the various kinds of romance between the young and the old? Or was she encouraging him, by letting him know that his interest was not all that unusual? In fact, it put him in rather distinguished company. Had that been her message?

It was impossible to think so, seeing her sitting so close to Hutton, bright-eyed, seemingly not that interested in the trial at all.

On the second day, Hanson flew up from Indianapolis and his testimony did Andrew little good.

"My conviction is based on what the medical examiners told me. If they are right, it cannot be said that death was by natural causes."

"You mean he was murdered?" Quarles said.

"His death was caused by someone, yes."

It was to that point that Andrew returned again and again when he questioned Hanson. The inspector had said to Quarles that a plastic bag might have had the effect the medical examiner discovered.

"What kind of plastic bag?"

"The kind shirts come from the laundry in."

"Were there shirts in Edgar's study in such bags?"

"Yes."

"Were any bags found other than those containing shirts?"

"One. In the wastebasket. It had contained the shirt the deceased was wearing."

"It could have been used in the way you are suggesting?"

"Yes. But it wasn't."

Andrew said he had found Hanson's testimony fascinating. "Let me sum it up and you tell me if I have left out anything. The medical examiner found evidence of deprivation of oxygen as well as of an infarction in the deceased. This suggests the possibility that someone was depriving Edgar of oxygen and this brought on the heart attack. Anyone trying to asphyxiate the old man and thereby causing his heart failure would be as guilty of the second as of the first. We are all agreed on that. We can also agree that a plastic bag pulled over the victim's head would suffice. But, Inspector Hanson, this is a trial

149

for murder and the defendant cannot be convicted by a possibility. Have you found a plastic bag that might have been used for this dreadful purpose?"

"No."

"So this is pure speculation."

"A plastic bag from the victim's closet is unaccounted for."

Andrew seemed delighted that Hanson had discovered that one shirt in the closet had been removed from its plastic bag and that plastic bag had not been found.

"You looked for it?"

"Of course."

"And did not find it?"

"No."

"Did you look in the garment bag in the closet."

"The garment bag?"

Andrew asked that a garment bag taken from Edgar Bissonet's closet be introduced as evidence. He then asked Hanson to unzip its pockets and search them. Hanson did this expressionlessly, and without result. He looked at Andrew.

"Try the section at the bottom reserved for shoes."

Hanson unzipped it, reached in, and brought forth a plastic bag.

"Is that the kind of bag you have been looking for, Inspector."

Hanson looked thoughtfully at Andrew. "Yes."

"It occurred to me, Inspector, that Edgar Bissonet might do what I myself do when traveling. Use a shirt bag as a laundry bag. I suppose your technicians could determine whether this one has been so used."

"Yes."

"Has this bag been examined?"

Andrew turned to Quarles, his brows raised in a question.

"I never saw the damned thing before," Quarles said.

"When I return from a trip and empty my improvised laundry bag, I often stuff it back in my garment bag. For future use. I suggest that this accounts for the missing bag and removes once and for all speculation about my client, or anyone else, pulling a bag over Edgar Bissonet's head."

Mintz, Quarles, and Hanson looked as if Andrew had pulled a bag over their heads. Or perhaps the wool over their eyes. But at adjournment, Foster noticed Andrew and Hanson in friendly conversation. When he joined them, he was surprised to hear Andrew say, "Of course this bag need not be the one missing from the closet. There's no way of telling how long it had been in Edgar's garment bag."

Hanson shook his head. "Whose side are you on, anyway?"

"Just because my client is innocent doesn't mean I don't want the murderer found."

"You need a murder in order to have a murderer. I believe those are your words."

"Yes. Yes they are and yes they are true."

TWENTY-FOUR

PATTY WAS CHANGING THE POSITION OF THE HOLE ON the fourteenth green and was just removing a plug of dirt when Andrew approached on foot from behind the green. She grinned in recognition, her mouth below the shadow cast by the bill of her cap. She looked back toward the tee and then in puzzlement at him.

"I'm not playing this hole."

"There wasn't one to play."

She put the metal cup into the ground from which she had removed the plug, then filled the former hole with the plug.

"I just played seven."

"You're lost?"

"Let's talk."

There was a bench on the fifteenth tee and she reluctantly accepted his suggestion that they use it. It was there that he had parked his cart, deciding that walking to where she was would be less alarming than suddenly appearing at the wheel of the cart.

He sat on the bench and somewhat to his surprise she lowered herself onto the grass. This had the disadvantage that unless she tipped her head far back he could not see her eyes.

"You couldn't have seen the seventh fairway or Edgar's house from the fifth."

"Did I say the fifth?"

He had considered this on the way over. He was certain she had said she was mowing the fifth that morning and looked back to see someone drive a cart onto the seventh fairway with what must have been Edgar's body.

"You want to change your testimony?"

Her head tipped back and calm eyes regarded him. "Is this a court?"

"It's what you'll be asked at the trial."

"How's it going?"

"Things look bad for Matthew Bissonet."

"Do you think he did it?"

"Tell me what you really saw that morning."

She rubbed her nose with the back of a hand from which she had removed a work glove.

152

"At the time, it seemed the right thing to do."

"Did you wave at Edgar when you were mowing the fairway behind his house?"

"I never thought of it as behind his house. The fairway was there first."

"Was he sitting on his patio that morning?"

The bill went up and down. Suddenly she took the hat off and her thick hair fell full to her shoulders. She shook it several times, then she put her arms straight out behind for support and looked him in the eye.

"I waved at him, but he didn't wave back. I thought he hadn't seen me, so I waved again when I was cutting the other way. That's when I noticed the shiny thing he was wearing over his head. The sunlight came and went on him because he was in the shade of a tree. There was the slightest breeze but it moved the branches so that when the sun hit the plastic it was like a flashing light."

"Plastic?"

"I stopped the mower when I came even with the patio and looked at him. After a while the leaves fluttered and again there was a reflection. I must have sat there for minutes before I decided to go see what was the matter. What the matter was was that he had pulled a plastic bag over his head. He was dead."

In her eyes the horror of that moment shone. Her eyes left his then and went out over the course as if in momentary commemoration of Edgar Bissonet. She drew her lower lip between her teeth; determined not to cry. Then she went on.

"I was surprised, in a way, when I read how old he was. He didn't seem that old to me. But I guess it seemed too old to him. Anyway, there he was, all dressed up for golf like most other mornings, only he wasn't going to do any more golfing. His last look must

153

have been at the course. Do you suppose he thought it would be the way they say it is with a killer, his victim's image imprinted on his eyes? Old Edgar really killed this course."

She smiled sadly and then the smile went but not the sadness.

"I guess I thought of the jokes about him, Gallagher's, Wirth's, most everybody else's. It didn't seem right that he should be found like that, sitting like a mummy, that plastic bag half hiding, half showing his face."

"So what did you do?"

"I took the bag off his head. That's all I meant to do. I think I was then going to call someone. But then I realized what I had done. I actually tried to put the bag back over his head again, but I couldn't do it. That's when I thought that it would be better if he was found out on the fairway."

"And you drove him out there."

"I sat next to him and got my leg across his and pushed the pedal. It was a straight shot out. On the way, I decided I would lay him on the ground, as if he had keeled over. That's what I did."

"Did you put the sand wedge in his hand?"

"Yes."

"It wasn't the right club."

The little smile flickered on her lips. "With him, it didn't matter."

"Did you have trouble getting the club into this hand?"

"Not really."

"What did you do with the plastic bag?"

She pushed forward and got into a squatting position, balancing herself easily. She pulled a few

154

blades of grass from the ground and brought them to her mouth.

"You play early. You know what a golf course is like in the morning."

"What time was this by the way?"

"I've thought about that. Six-thirty, in around there."

"What about the golf course in the early morning?"

"I did all that and I never once imagined anyone would see me do it." She shook her head in disbelief. "At that hour, you just assume the world is all yours, certainly the golf course. Oh, I had seen Mr. Wirth earlier, heading for the clubhouse as he does every morning, but that's like the sun coming up. So there was that. I just moved him from his patio to the fairway and never once worried that I'd be seen. And then, when I had him laid out, I stayed around. It seemed there should be a little ceremony."

"You said a prayer?"

She was embarrassed. "It seemed the right thing."

"What did you say?"

She glanced at him but didn't quite meet his eye. "Do you know, 'Now I lay me down to sleep'?"

" 'I pray to God my soul to keep.' "

"That's the one. I said all that, standing over him, but it didn't seem enough. So I decided to bury the plastic bag. To get rid of it, but also to . . ." She closed her eyes and made a face. "I don't know." She looked up. "That was a terrible thing to do, wasn't it?"

"Where did you bury it?"

"In the trap."

"Why don't we go over there to see if it's there?"

She lifted herself effortlessly from her crouched position.

"In a minute."

155

"What made you think Edgar himself had put that bag over his head?"

She thought about it, running her fingers over the clubs emerging from the bag strapped to the back of Andrew's cart.

"Because he was all alone?"

"Any other reason?"

She had pulled a wedge from his bag and was gripping it. "You think someone else did it?"

"It's possible, isn't it?"

"And maybe was still around and watched me while I moved him?"

He let her think about it herself. That she had come upon a suicide seemed simply to have been her unexamined thought. She couldn't think of any specific reason why she had come to that conclusion. She had taken a stance and was bringing the club back. Her follow-through was easy, head down, and the club head slipped through the grass at her feet. Andrew took a ball from his pocket and tossed it. It came to a stop before her. She looked toward the green where she had just changed the position of the hole, she looked at the ball, she concentrated. Then the club was taken back smoothly, slowly and, in a continuous rhythm, returned to the ball. Her body weight shifted, the ball rose in a perfect arc and landed on the green.

"Where'd it end up?" he asked.

"I can't see."

"You're a natural golfer."

She handed him the club. "You hit one."

He dropped a ball and hit it and then they walked to the green. There was a ball in the fringe, where it must have rolled after landing on the sloping green. Andrew went to it.

"This is mine."

"I don't see the other."

"Look in the hole."

"Come on."

"Look."

She cried out when she did look, stooping to pluck the ball out, but her smile faded.

"What kind of ball did you hit?"

"A Golden Bear."

"That's what this is."

"It's the only kind I use."

"But how do we know whose ball went in the hole?"

"It had to be yours. I know I was long."

"I want to believe that, but how can I know for sure?"

"I'm sure. I saw your hit and felt mine. I was long. Obviously you weren't."

"If it hadn't gone in, it might have run off the green."

"That's true."

She would take her own cart to the sand trap on the seventh hole and Andrew would follow. Actually, she drove slowly until he caught up.

"I'll never be sure I chipped in that ball," she said.

He let it go. He wasn't that sure himself and it was silly to think that one golfer could confer such a result on another. Andrew felt he had hit his ball a tad too strongly but the fact was that neither of them had been able to see the result of their shots.

"You'll be making many shots like that, Patty."

"Are we still going to have a round?"

"As soon as the trial is over."

At the bunker in the seventh fairway, they waited for a trio of women to play through. One pair of sunglasses under a jaunty straw hat took particular notice of Andrew and Patty. Patty was wearing her cap again, but her long hair still hung to her shoulders. Andrew waved at the sunglasses and got a tentative wave in reply.

They waited until the women had made their approach shots to the green and then Patty stepped into the trap.

"It was right here."

"You're that sure?"

"I triangulated it. Edgar's patio door, the bench on the tee, and that willow."

She pushed away sand with her shoe and then knelt to use her hands. Soon a corner of a clear plastic bag became visible.

"Cover it up again," Andrew said.

"You don't want it?"

"I want to know it's there. It's best to let it be for now."

"I hope you were right," Patty said, when she was once again behind the wheel of her cart, the sand raked back into uniformity.

"Patty, I know it was your ball."

She laughed. "I meant about Edgar not committing suicide. I'm sure you are. But I didn't want anyone thinking so. He was killed."

TWENTY-FIVE

SUSANNAH TOOK THE CALL WHEN ELENA TELEPHONED to say that the disk containing Edgar Bissonet's autobiography had arrived from Santiago.

"Can you bring it here?"

"It's only one disk. I had it transferred by E-mail from Chile. What is your Internet number?"

Susannah confessed they did not have one. Neither she

nor Andrew had been quite sure what the advantages were when Gerald had urged it on them.

"I don't suppose you can fax it."

"It would have to be printed out first. And it is very long."

"I'll come pick it up."

"I'm calling from Muncie."

"Muncie!"

"I'm visiting a friend at Ball State."

"How long will you be there?"

"Oh, I really shouldn't have come here, I suppose. Because of the trial. I'll be back in Wyler tomorrow. When does the morning session begin?"

"Nine-thirty."

"I wanted to talk to Andrew about the autobiography before giving it to him."

"Could you come here at nine in the morning?"

"Nine o'clock," Elena murmured, obviously not liking the thought of how early she would have to get up to make that appointment.

"Or you could talk after the morning session."

"But what if I'm called to the stand in the morning?"

"Do you have to talk to Andrew?"

"What do you mean?"

Susannah didn't like to send Gerald on a drive to Muncie but she did, figuring if he couldn't go she would make the trip herself. In compensation, she took Julie to lunch.

"I hope this has nothing to do with Gerald," Julie said.

"Gerald?"

"So it does."

"You're jumping to conclusions."

The lunch put Susannah in an equivocal position. She

understood Andrew's opposition to Gerald's attraction to Julie but she also understood Gerald's attraction. The suggestion that opposing it added another powerful factor to the situation was dismissed by Andrew.

"I've seen them together."

"Andrew, you can't blame Gerald."

"He's putty in her hands, that's obvious. I think he thought she was just a small-town girl but he is up against a very shrewd young lady."

"What are you saying?"

"She's after him. I wouldn't be surprised if Frank hadn't put her up to it."

"Andrew, that is preposterous. It is Gerald who is pursuing her."

"I suppose it looks that way. He probably believes that's the way it is."

"When in the world did you become such a chauvinist?"

"I don't like to see him made a fool of."

There are some conversations it is pointless to continue and that had been one of them. This attitude was completely uncharacteristic of Andrew, but then Gerald was the only nephew he had. He had explained to Gerald the old enmity between himself and Frank McGough, assuming that would suffice. Gerald had told Susannah that Julie had received an identical warning from her father. Obviously such considerations did not weigh heavily on either of them.

Susannah was kept more or less informed of the progress of Gerald's pursuit. Fortunately, Andrew had no idea how often Gerald and Julie saw one another. It was a serious attraction and opposition only added zest to something that was in itself already sufficiently attractive. Gerald had all but begged her to explain to

Julie about his lunches with Louella and with Rebecca.

"Gerald, it might help to have her a little jealous."

"What makes you so sure it's only a little?"

"Why didn't you just tell her it was part of your work?"

"You would have had to be there to understand why I couldn't do that."

"Is there something for her to be jealous of?" Susannah asked delicately.

"You would be the first to know."

"That's not an answer."

"What would count toward an answer?"

He was teasing her, of course. Was that in his genes or had he picked it up from his uncle Andrew?

"Gerald, I am not going to plead your case if you are just playing a game with her and with me. I should be discouraging your interest in Julie, not the reverse."

He took her in his arms and held her close. "Do this for me and I will name our first daughter Susannah."

One of Susannah's crosses was that she was unlikely to bear any children of her own, given her own age if not Andrew's. The papers were full of stories nowadays of women resorting to extraordinary means to bear children—grandmothers providing a womb in which their grandchildren might develop, wives impregnated with the seed of men other than their husbands, couples able to do with technical assistance what they could not do in the privacy of their bedrooms. Andrew had never expressed the least interest in any of this, much to Susannah's relief. She found such resorts aesthetically unattractive as well as against the teaching of her church. Andrew obviously saw Gerald as the son he would never have, and Susannah now realized how susceptible she was to the suggestion that Gerald's children would be hers at one remove.

And so she went off to lunch with Julie. It took half an hour before Julie would even acknowledge that Gerald had done anything to peeve her.

"He dreads the thought that there is someone else."

"Someone else!" The emotion that flickered across Julie's face enlivened her beauty.

"Maybe you're not as serious about him as he is with you."

Julie leaned over the table with narrowed flashing eyes. "When has he seen me fawning over any man the way I saw him groveling before two different women?"

"Julie, he was working on the Bissonet case."

"He was having the time of his life."

"He was trying to get the cooperation of two extremely important sources of information if Matthew Bissonet is to be acquitted."

Julie reacted as if this had never occurred to her. She tapped her lower teeth with a breadstick, looking at Susannah. And then abruptly the storm seemed over.

"Is he innocent?"

She meant Matthew.

"He wouldn't harm a fly."

"Physically maybe. But he has lost money for people. But that would be a reason to harm him, not his father. It's no secret that he has all but ruined his father's firm."

Talking about the trial and the case against Matthew provided the most natural way to accomplish her mission of showing that Gerald's lunch with Louella had been an effort to gain better knowledge of the workings of Matthew's brokerage firm.

"And you know how important it is to keep the press on one's side."

"The press."

"Gerald said he saw you when he was lunching in the Roundball with Rebecca Prell of the *Dealer.*"

"That child is a reporter?"

"Fred Foster says she is one of his best."

Julie remembered something and her anger was back. "But he lied to me, Susannah. He had that girl seated at a booth in the lounge and he told me he was going elsewhere for lunch."

"You have to see that in the light of his fear that you would misunderstand. Of course he should simply have explained what was going on. He sees that now. He saw it a few minutes after he spoke with you."

"Does he really think I'm going with someone else?"

"I told him he doesn't own you. It isn't as if you were engaged."

"You know my father."

"I know his uncle."

"Why do things have to be so complicated?"

"The two of you will work it out, I'm sure of it."

"Are you on our side?"

"We're having lunch, aren't we?"

She did not like to say flat out that she opposed Andrew's view of the situation. Gerald had asked her what, beyond a general rivalry, underlay Andrew's antipathy to Frank. The specific incidents she could come up with had not seemed to him sufficient explanation. It appeared that Julie too did not understand why misunderstandings between her father and Andrew should stand in the way of her happiness. Susannah was certain the feud was not as irrational as it seemed and she had long since given up hope that it would simply go away. Knowing that, she had put

163

herself in an equivocal position smoothing Julie's feathers for Gerald and even aligning herself with their cause.

"I don't want to elope. I want a big wedding."

"It will be the event of the decade in Wyler."

Julie beamed and it seemed cruel to make the dream of that great social event an impossible one. Her expression was sad when she asked where Gerald was as they lunched.

"On his way to Muncie."

"What for?"

Susannah put a finger to her lips. "Let's just say it's connected with Matthew Bissonet's trial."

"If there's another woman involved, I'll brain him."

Susannah thought of the fiery beauty of Elena. If Julie had been made angry by Gerald's being with Louella and with Rebecca, the sight of him with Elena would set off real fireworks.

"You're even more beautiful when you're jealous."

TWENTY-SIX

WHEN HE GOT TO MUNCIE AFTER A MEDITATIVE DRIVE over secondary roads that wended their way through the fields of Indiana, Gerald called the number he had been given by Susannah and a man answered.

"Is Elena there?"

"Who's calling?"

"Is that you, Hector?"

Silence.

"Hector?"

A hand over the receiver did not quite suppress the sound of voices and then Elena came on.

"This is Gerald Rowan. I'm supposed to pick up a disk?"

"Hector doesn't want me to turn it over."

"How do I get to where you are?"

"Are you in Muncie?"

"Yes."

"Come to the campus of Ball State."

He nodded through the instructions, hung up, and went out to his car. Had he come all this way for nothing? It was difficult to resent the pleasant drive during which he had entertained himself with thoughts of how Susannah would persuade Julie of his professional self-sacrifice in lunching with Louella and Rebecca. He had hardly noticed that either one of them might drive men mad, so intent had he been on amassing information favorable to the defense of Matthew Bissonet. Why even as they spoke he was choking in the exhaust from semis, sacrificing lunch in order to retrieve the sole copy of Edgar Bissonet's autobiography . . . In his fantasy, Julie wept helplessly, Susannah assured her that her doubts would be forgiven her, and the two women set about elaborate preparations for his return.

In the unfanciful streets of Muncie, he wondered if he should regard Hector as friend or foe. Elena had no obligation to turn over the disk containing the autobiography she had written down at Edgar's dictation. Should she at Hector's behest renege on her promise, she might be keeping from the trial more embarrassing information about the testy relations between Matthew and his father. The computer file had dropped down the black hole of memory, along with the file containing the love poems the old man had written for his secretary and which she had entered into his computer. Of those, however, she said she had retained the handwritten originals. But the poems, whatever the case of the autobiography, presented unequivocal difficulties for the defense in the case of *State of Indiana v. Matthew Bissonet.*

Andrew's taste in poetry had made him susceptible to the rather traditional forms Edgar's effusions to Elena had taken—the stanzas, the language, suggested the early volumes in the collections that had followed Gerald through college, poems of earlier centuries, unlike the authors he preferred— Stevens, Lowell, Snodgrass. The point of the earlier stuff was to prepare the way for Gerald's poets. But old-fashioned or not, the poems revealed an old fool drooling over Elena, expressing his love in sometimes eye-popping sensuousness, more often in honeyed circumlocution.

In any case, the poems were proof that Matthew's suspicion about his father's susceptibility to Elena was well founded. Any old man who could send such poems was fully capable of making Elena his heir, as indeed he had.

Louise Schwartz had tucked in her chin and looked at Gerald over the tops of her glasses.

"Yes?"

The barest of nods. Gerald was reflecting that Louise was a very attractive widow who should not be wasting her life rescuing Judge Mintz from the consequences of his incompetence. But then the effect of her Spanish olive eyes and alabaster skin gave way to the fact that Edgar had indeed already included Elena in his will.

"Spanish olive eyes?" Susannah had said when Gerald had told her.

"Alabaster skin?" came from Andrew's office.

Susannah said, "You have come under the spell of Edgar's verse."

Gerald sentenced himself to an evening rinsing out his mind with Panovsky's postmodern pyrotechnics. Andrew responded to Gerald's account of Louise's reaction to Edgar's will with indifference. They had already known of the change. The change exculpated Matthew rather than the reverse. Gerald was finding it difficult to share his uncle's continued confidence that the case against Matthew was weak. The weakness depended on things which might not enter into the trial—the autobiography, the poems, and Elena's inclusion in Edgar's will—any one of which would bolster Quarles's contention that the bad blood between father and son provided ample motivation for parricide. And if Andrew was serious about putting Matthew on the stand, their client would be condemned out of his own mouth when he described threatening Edgar, and tearing up his study in a search for the will.

Would Hector prevent Elena from turning over to Matthew's defenders the sole copy of Edgar's autobiography? Gerald was determined to prevent that.

The campus of Ball State contrasted with the scrunched and crowded campuses where land was at a premium, each acre pressed into service. Here there were wide vistas, expanses of lawn, a sense of spaciousness under the elms and oaks and beeches. There was no sign of Elena when he entered the circular drive to which she had directed him. He parked and, resting his arms on the wheel, was searching the horizon when there was a tap on the back window. He saw her first in the side mirror but then she scampered around the front of the car to the passenger seat. Her blouse was pulled back from one shoulder, her skirt looked as if she had twisted it to the side, there was a wild hunted look on her face. Instinctively Gerald leaned to his right and pushed open the passenger door and she slipped in and began to pull it closed when she was prevented from doing so by an equally wild-eyed Hector. Elena was crying and cursing in a language the stranger does not know.

Gerald pushed his door open, went around to the passenger side, grabbed Hector's shoulder, and spun him around. There were trails of blood down the young man's cheek from what appeared to be scratches. His black hair fell across his forehead, his tailored shirt hung outside his trousers as if he, like Elena, had come in unseemly haste to this rendezvous. Hector, spitting invective in Spanish, swung his free arm at Gerald, who grabbed his wrist and used the force of the blow to bring Hector's arm up behind him as he turned. The young man cried out in pain.

"In his pocket," Elena cried, looking up at him through the window of the closed passenger door of his car. "He has the disk in his pocket."

Still crying out with pain, Hector took something from his shirt pocket and sailed it far out into the circular pool that formed the hub around which the drive circled. Gerald watched the computer disk as if in slow motion describe a great trajectory from Hector's flinging fingers to the pool and then sink beneath the water. Even as he did so, thoughts of Norton Utilities came to him, the program that enabled one to retrieve erased files from a computer. Files that had once been on Edgar's computer could be brought back from oblivion. Consequently, he gave Hector a disdainful push, got behind the wheel of his car, and locked all the doors. But it was the windshield Hector decided to beat upon. He flung himself across the hood of the car, looking with beseeching rage at Elena, pounding on the glass that separated them. Gerald put the car in motion and immediately Elena began to scream at him to stop.

"He'll kill himself," she cried. "You'll kill him."

But under the centrifugal force of Gerald's accelerated movement along the curved drive, Hector began to slide from the hood. He grabbed at the windshield wiper, which provided no grip at all, and soon he and the wiper slid completely off. Gerald turned sharply away from the curb and caught a glimpse of Hector sitting on the edge of the drive, shaking the windshield wiper in ineffectual rage.

"He's all right," he assured Elena.

"He's a fool!"

"Well, you know him better than I do."

She burst into tears and that seemed a fitting end to the fracas. She was saying she must go back to him, but he countered with the repetition of the judgment that Hector was a fool. This impassioned dialogue continued as Gerald headed out of Muncie.

"Where are you taking me?"

The question had the making of an accusation. He turned into a franchise food place and found a parking space.

"I can't be seen like this," Elena said, tugging at her clothes and peering at herself in the little mirror in the back of the sun guard she had lowered.

"Use the rest room."

"Thank you," she said, and got out of the car and hurried to the side door. Gerald slumped in his seat, wondering if he shouldn't just leave, abandoning the fiery Elena to her own devices. His version of what had happened was that he had rescued her from her witless

169

lover. She had just suggested that he was forcibly removing her. He compromised by changing parking spaces.

Ten minutes later, Elena emerged transformed. Her hair was brushed, her clothes no longer disordered. She looked around with the confidence of a beauty who feels the eyes of the world upon her. Then she spied the car and came toward it not only voluntarily but in a way that captured the attention of most males in the immediate vicinity.

"Did you move?"

"I was going to abandon you here."

Her incredulous laugh rose in a sensuous gargle as she settled in the seat beside him.

"I'm heading back to Wyler."

"Of course."

"You're coming with me?"

"I must. The only place Edgar's autobiography exists now is here."

She tapped her forehead with a painted nail and smiled in a way that Julie might have found suggestive.

He drove out of the lot and turned in the direction of Wyler. No need to tell her that he could retrieve the erased files from Edgar's hard drive. He said, "We can stop for lunch on the way."

"I couldn't eat."

"You can watch me. I missed lunch coming over here."

"Oh." She put a hand on his arm. "I'm so sorry."

"Why was Hector against your letting Andrew have the autobiography?"

She made a little puffing sound. "It was the poems that made him angry. Oh, he is such an idiot. He burned them!"

"You can't blame him for being jealous."

"Jealous! Why should he be jealous?" But she smiled gleefully at the thought.

"I've seen those poems, Elena. Hector obviously loves you. No man would enjoy the thought that the woman he loved had received such poems from another man, let alone . . ."

"I didn't *receive* those poems."

"But they were written for you."

Her laughter rode up and down the scale, delighted, derisory, surprised. There were tears in her eyes as she laughed.

"You thought Edgar sent those poems to me!"

"Your name figures in most of them," Gerald said defensively.

"He wrote them to my mother!"

TWENTY-SEVEN

TALKING WITH STAN TRUMBLE WAS PAINFUL BUT Rebecca bit the bullet and called the broker. She had been surprised he hadn't been in court, given his chatty vindictiveness when he spoke about his employer. It was something Matthew's wife had said that decided Rebecca to grit her teeth and call on Trumble.

"Edgar hired him and Matthew kept him on against his better judgment."

"I understood he was pretty good."

"You've been talking with him."

Rebecca smiled. "He isn't bashful."

"Edgar warned Matthew about him, but Matthew didn't think he had anything to learn from his father."

"Warned him?"

"Sharp practices. I don't understand any of it, but I understand when someone is being called a crook. He still owed Edgar money, but most of all he owed him for not having him drummed out of the business."

It could have been merely the accused's wife trying to divert attention from her husband, except that Claire clearly considered the trial a giant mistake that would inevitably be corrected. Matthew would never have struck his father, let alone killed him.

"Shouting at him was as far as he could go."

Rebecca did not remind Claire of the torn-up study. This confidence plus Foster's efforts to pursue the spoor of Elena's possible guilt convinced Rebecca to call on Trumble. But first she called Louella and suggested drinks at the Roundball when the office closed.

"All the men in here are married or worse," Louella said knowledgeably.

"What's worse?"

"Pretending they're not."

"Where do such eligible males as Trumble hang out?"

"Eligible!"

"He's single, isn't he?"

"Who would marry such a monster?"

"Obviously you have no crush on your boss."

"He is not my boss. I wish he would get run over some morning when he's out running."

"He runs?"

"Can you believe it? A pudge like that."

Rebecca verified it the next morning, parking her Cherokee in the lot of Trumble's condo, waiting for him to emerge. He was all in black, even his shoes and sweatband, and he wore dark glasses. Few people were recognizable when out running, at least in Rebecca's experience, but Trumble seemed determined to be

172

incognito. Rebecca gave him a block lead and then fell into a rhythmic jog behind him, keeping the interval. He did not look around, of course, why would he? There is nothing more solitary than running. She was not prepared for the extent of his run. He cut diagonally across a school playground, gained the county road, and settled down for what was obviously miles and miles of running. At the country club, he went past the entrance and turned onto a narrow road. It was then that Rebecca realized that the houses on their left were those built on the edge of the golf course. When she passed Edgar's house and then Matthew's, what Claire had told her took on a new significance. It was three hours later that she dropped by the brokerage.

In the absence of Matthew, Trumble's manner had become proprietary and he barked orders right and left with uncontested authority. But he was all smiles when Louella led Rebecca in to him.

"Isn't this Matthew's office?"

"What a wonderful memory you have." He waved her grandly to a chair and sat behind the desk, glancing at the monitor of his computer before giving her his full attention.

"Busy?"

"The market never sleeps."

"Do you always get up at five?"

"Always."

"You begin your run at five-twenty. I assume you have been up for a minute or two."

"Do you run?"

"Not as far as you do."

He wrinkled his nose. "I have the impression you are informing me about myself."

"Well, after all, there was bad blood between you and

a murder victim and I'm covering the trial."

"What on earth are you talking about?"

"The Bissonets have been fairly vague about it, of course, but I suspect it will all come out sooner or later."

He studied her for a moment. His welcoming manner was gone and he had more of the look of a usurper of the throne.

"What would come out, as you put it, is that I have been a very valuable employee for both of the Bissonets."

"I wouldn't expect you to share their point of view."

Trumble moved a finger back and forth along his upper lip. "I suppose a man who is cornered will strike out at anyone."

"Matthew insists he is innocent."

"Then he should be acquitted."

"Andrew Broom is certain he will be."

"Well then, things will be as they were."

"Not quite. There is still a murder to be accounted for."

"I think the police will know where to look. If there is an associate of Edgar's on whom suspicion might fall, it is certainly not I."

"Elena?"

"Bingo."

"Did you see her out there that morning?"

He leaned forward, frowning.

"On your run past the Bissonets'. I would advise against saying you did, since she can show she was nowhere near Edgar's house. You on the other hand were seen in the neighborhood."

By Rebecca, a few hours before, that is. Suddenly his manner changed. He put his elbows on the desk and seemed to catch his chin just before it might have bounced off the ink blotter.

"How do you know these things?"

Rebecca was unprepared for this sudden collapse on the part of the hitherto cocky Trumble. Good God, was he going to confess? Apparently not. He begged her to believe he had done nothing to harm Edgar Bissonet, no matter what his son might think.

"The old man could have ruined me." His eyes darted about in search of a way to put it. "I engaged in some indiscreet practices, nothing wrong, really, but open to misunderstanding. And I found myself unable to meet some serious margin calls. Edgar came to my rescue. Is it likely that I would do harm to the man, and after all this time?"

"But you did run past his house on the morning he was found dead?"

"It was no different from any other morning."

"Nothing out of the ordinary?"

He looked tragically at her. "You wouldn't believe me."

Rebecca waited.

"I saw Matthew on the fairway, going from his father's house to his own. If he even noticed me he wouldn't have recognized me."

"Are you sure you didn't read that in the paper?"

"I said you wouldn't believe me."

"It *was* in the paper."

"I read only the financial news and I am unlikely to rely on the *Dealer* for that."

With this put-down some of his usual bravura returned. Until he sought assurance that no one other than Rebecca had placed him near the house the morning Edgar was found dead.

"God only knows what crimes and misdemeanors I run past in the course of a morning."

"If Matthew didn't kill Edgar, someone must have."

"No one had a better motive than Elena. But you say she can account for her whereabouts." An idea clicked and his expression altered. "She needn't have done it herself, you know. It could have been that boyfriend of hers."

"How much do you still owe Edgar?"

"I never missed a payment!"

He half rose as he said this. Rebecca left then, leaving a suitably unhinged Trumble to wonder what kind of trouble he might be in.

TWENTY-EIGHT

UNLIKE HIS OFFICE, WHICH GAVE HIM A PANORAMIC view of the surrounding countryside, Andrew Broom's study was located in the basement of his home and had no window on the world whatsoever. In it, pure concentration was possible. He had weaned himself from the notion that he required certain conditions in which to work, but some circumstances are better than others. His home study was the ideal place to prepare for court and there, very early in the morning of the day when he would open the defense of Matthew Bissonet, he sat reviewing the printout Gerald had dropped by the night before.

"The autobiography."

"Elena provided it?"

"Not quite. Her paramour, if that's what he is, sailed it into a reflecting pool. At that very moment I thought of the merits of Norton Utilities."

"A stock?"

"A computer program that enables one to retrieve erased files."

With the program, Gerald had recovered from electronic limbo the files containing the autobiography Edgar had been dictating to Elena Maria. The document contained fewer surprises because of Gerald's discovery of the true dedicatee of Edgar's poems.

"Her mother! Check that out, will you?"

A fax from associates in Santiago was among the materials Andrew had before him for review. It confirmed that Elena Maria's mother was indeed a resident of that city, and a member of a wealthy and prominent family. No doubt, the same associates could establish the woman's sojourn in the States when she had engaged in a liaison with Edgar Bissonet. That bittersweet affair was the remote object toward which Edgar's autobiography had been moving, the *fons et origo* which explained Elena's existence. Its style was cloying and cutesy, difficult to associate with Edgar, but then what must be the emotions of an old man when being reunited with his natural daughter, a young woman who showed him a good deal more affection and respect and devotion than his legitimate children did? Of course in Chile Elena was considered a legitimate child, the daughter of the late Edgar Bissonet of Wyler, Indiana. Elena's reunion with her allegedly deceased father had obviously been a joy and satisfaction to both of them.

In a memo, Gerald summed up what he had learned from Rebecca Prell about Stanley Trumble's morning jog, as well as the broker's plaintive suggestion that Hector Sonora had far more motive than Stan—after all, Hector was a hot-blooded Latin who improbably considered Edgar a rival for the affections of Elena Maria.

Andrew closed his eyes, pushed back from the desk, and reviewed the case Cecil Quarles had made against Matthew. It was admittedly circumstantial, but this was Indiana, not California, and jurors were less likely to dismiss the logic of the prosecutor's argument.

Edgar Bissonet was dead and not of natural causes. Matthew Bissonet, floundering in the brokerage his father had bequeathed him, was upset that his aging father had made Elena Maria the principal beneficiary of his will. Not only would this be hard on Matthew's children, as well as their cousins, but it would take away cash on which Matthew counted to make up for bad judgments of his own. Matthew's interest in his father's will was manifest in his admitted argument with the old man on the very morning of Edgar's death and then in his tearing up the study and consulting his father's computer in search of notes Edgar claimed to have made concerning the redrafting of his will. Greed and jealousy had led Matthew, in a rage, to pull a plastic bag over his father's head and leave him sitting on his patio. The plastic bag had not been produced but Andrew Broom knew where it was and he had a solemn obligation to produce it in evidence. To fulfill that obligation would seemingly deliver the coup de grace to his client.

Andrew had faced difficult assignments before, and he had welcomed them, wanting the challenge to his forensic skills and lawyerly expertise. He felt now a prisoner of his success. And of his confident boasting to Gerald and Susannah. There had been a point when he feared that Matthew would admit to him his guilt. At the moment, he almost wished he had. But he was certain Matthew was innocent. Failure to gain an acquittal for a client he knew to be guilty would be considerably easier to bear. But Andrew Broom had no doubt that Matthew was innocent of his father's death. His certainty came from everything he knew of Matthew and his family. It would be a revelation to many that the members of one of Wyler's preeminent families quarreled among themselves as others do. But Matthew's denial of wrongdoing, at least that for which he was standing trial, convinced Andrew. How could he convey that certainty to the jury?

Watching them during the preceding days of the trial, both during court sessions and as they entered and left the jury box, Andrew detected a faint sense of underdog triumphalism, particularly in Gabe Conway, the foreman. Gabe's father had been the town drunk; Gabe himself ran a successful plumbing and heating business and was a legendary softball pitcher. After he installed the plumbing and heating in Edgar's house, the old man had contested the bill and it had been necessary to do a lot of negotiation with Nancy Sewell, Gabe's attorney, to achieve a satisfactory settlement. There had been no point in bringing this up during the selection of the jury as it would have suggested possible sympathy with the defendant, and indeed Andrew at the time had thought that might be the case. But Gabe's manner, which seemed infectious with the other jurors, was that of a man conscious that he might play a role in seeing that justice was done to the Bissonet family. Things looked dark indeed. Andrew returned to his study of the materials before him.

His motion for dismissal having been denied, Andrew set about the careful scenario he had worked out earlier. Patty Cermac, looking surprisingly girlish in an olive-green dress that emphasized her tanned skin and sun-

179

streaked hair, took the stand with obvious reluctance, but as Andrew led her through the questions he had rehearsed with her, she relaxed. He established the time when she had begun mowing Number Nine, putting her on the seventh fairway at seven o'clock or only slightly earlier.

"You can see the Edgar Bissonet home from that fairway, can't you?"

"There are half a dozen homes built on the edge of the seventh fairway."

"Among them Edgar Bissonet's?"

"Yes."

"Did you know him?"

"I talked with him on several occasions. He liked to hit balls around on the seventh fairway."

"Could he come onto it from his house?"

"He had a golf cart and he would drive it on and hit balls back and forth."

"Was he doing that on the morning of July 17?"

"No."

"Did you see him that morning?"

"Yes."

"Describe to the court what you saw."

When Patty began, Cecil Quarles and his associates settled back, prepared to hear Patty describe waving to Edgar and then later, from the fifth fairway, seeing him driven onto the golf course. Her testimony now was the true account of how she had gone to Edgar when he failed to respond to her and then found him with a plastic bag pulled over his head.

"I took if off," Patty said when Andrew asked what she had then done.

"Why did you do that?"

"I didn't want him found that way."

"With the plastic bag over his head. What did you take to be the bag's significance?"

"I thought he had committed suicide."

"And you wanted to spare the family the embarrassment of such a death?"

"I don't know the family. Mr. Bissonet had always been so nice to me, I thought it would be better if it looked as if he had died of a heart attack or something. I didn't think the death of someone that old would surprise anyone."

"And you got rid of the plastic bag?"

"Yes.

"On the course?"

"Yes."

Quarles let Blake cross-examine and he spent the time establishing that Patty's testimony contradicted her pretrial deposition, something Andrew was willing to stipulate, but Blake pursued it relentlessly, since it called into question the reliability of the witness.

"I don't see what difference it makes," Mintz opined. "Either way, Edgar Bissonet's dead. It's how he got that way that we are concerned with here. If you want to bring charges against this young lady for carting a dead body around, that's another matter."

Quarles intervened. "Your Honor is perfectly right, of course. Whatever this young woman did to obscure what Matthew Bissonet had done is ultimately irrelevant."

Andrew then called Stanley Trumble and spent half an hour establishing that Trumble had been hired by Edgar but continued with Bissonet Brokers after Matthew took over. How would Trumble describe the relationship between father and son? Quarles half rose from his seat, then subsided.

"Oedipal," Stanley said.

"What was that?" Mintz demanded.

"He had an Oedipus complex, like most sons."

Mintz wanted to know what in blazes the witness was talking about. Quarles could not resist the opportunity. "It is a psychiatric theory according to which sons wish to kill their fathers. The witness is attributing such a wish to the defendant."

Quarles had thrown back his shoulders and now surveyed the courtroom with enormous self-satisfaction. It is not often that the prosecutor has his work done for him by the defense attorney, he seemed to be saying. In that arena, where Andrew Broom had known nothing but victory, it was understandable that Cecil should wish to anticipate what he clearly foresaw as a personal triumph.

Andrew let Cecil have his moment, then returned to questioning his witness.

"You know the location of Edgar Bissonet's home, Mr. Trumble?"

"Yes."

"Have you ever been there?"

"Inside? Once, I think."

"Recently?"

"Oh no. This was not long after Mr. Bissonet retired."

"And you haven't been there since?"

"Not inside, no."

And so they went on to Stanley's morning jog and his passing the Edgar Bissonet home on the morning of July 17. Had he noticed anything significant? He had seen the defendant passing from his father's house to his own.

"Ah. I wonder what time that would have been?"

Quarles objected that the prosecution had established

182

this when Alice Fritz was on the stand, but Andrew was told to proceed. He repeated his question to Trumble.

"Before six, perhaps five minutes before."

"You can be that precise?"

"I run the same route every morning. At that time I am just about at midpoint and will be turning back. The time does not vary more than five minutes from run to run."

"So it is no mere guess on your part that it was before 6 A.M. on July 17 when you saw Matthew Bissonet going from his father's house to his own?"

"No. That's when I saw him."

"Thank you, Mr. Trumble."

Quarles let Konstantin examine the witness, and the deputy prosecutor dwelled on the tension and disagreements between father and son.

That was the case for the defense. Andrew sensed the unease in Gerald when he returned to the table. Mintz was delighted at the brevity of Andrew's case and suggested immediate summaries so that he could charge the jury.

Quarles reviewed the case he had made, but concentrated on what the defense had brought forth.

"No doubt the defense attorney was as surprised as I was at Miss Cermac's change of testimony, but he apparently regarded it as somehow deflecting attention from his client. Judge Mintz made clear that, however shocking the young woman's actions in driving a corpse onto the golf course and laying it on the grass, this changes absolutely nothing. The defense has also conveniently made clear that there was animosity between the defendant and his father. The motive is there, the crime has been committed, and the defendant was on the scene. I ask the jury to return a verdict of guilty."

Cecil wisely adopted a rueful tone toward the end, speaking more in sorrow than in anger, and then walked slowly to his chair, with his chin on his chest. Andrew waited until Cecil was seated, then got to his feet and walked swiftly to the jury box.

"I shall be brief, ladies and gentlemen, and I ask you to forgive me for pointing out what I am sure is already obvious to you. Testimony given in this courtroom establishes beyond the shadow of a doubt that Matthew Bissonet could not have killed his father, whatever semblance of motive on his part, whatever provocation on his father's. You heard Dr. Whelper testify that death occurred between six-twenty and six twenty-five. Patty Cermac, while mowing the seventh fairway noticed Edgar Bissonet sitting on the patio of his house with a plastic bag over his head. And you have heard Stanley Trumble testify that he saw Matthew going from Edgar's house to his own at approximately six o'clock. Put these three together and we see that Matthew had left his father's house at least twenty minutes before Edgar died. If nothing else, these three facts, testified to under oath and uncontested by the prosecution, undermine the prosecution's effort to establish beyond reasonable doubt that Matthew Bissonet killed his father. I confidently await your verdict of not guilty."

Mintz waved off Cecil Quarles's effort to rebut Andrew's summary and began instructing the jury. Watching a dozen citizens leave the courtroom with Gabe in their lead, Andrew almost felt the confidence he had expressed. Susannah squeezed his arm, Gerald shook his head in admiration, Andrew swept papers into his briefcase.

"Let's get out of here."

"I don't think we should go far," Susannah said. "The jury isn't going to need much time."

But two days of deliberation lay ahead, during which Andrew responded to Gerald's and Susannah's question as to what the devil was taking them so long.

"Someone will have pointed out that Matthew could have gone back to his father's house."

"But there's no testimony to that effect."

"Jurors are ordinary citizens, not lawyers. Once they go into that room, their word is more powerful than law. If they say Matthew is guilty, then he is guilty."

"But Matthew didn't kill his father."

"No, he didn't."

"Cecil Quarles did not prove that he did it."

"No, he didn't."

No matter how they were instructed, the jurors would apply the same criteria to the defense as they did to the prosecution. It could be shown in a million ways that the argument Andrew had mounted on the three times testified to did not prove that Matthew had not killed his father. All it proved was that the testimony did not establish his guilt. That proving a negative fact is logically impossible would not occur to the jury. Andrew's argument would look as inconclusive as Cecil's. Their decision would be based on all those hidden factors that make human beings individuals, interesting and unpredictable.

On the third day, the jury arrived at a verdict. Court was reconvened, the atmosphere was solemn, Judge Mintz asked Gabe Conroy if they had reached a verdict. They had. Louise Schwartz, acting as bailiff, handed the envelope to the judge. He opened it with great

185

deliberation and read it silently but with moving lips. He turned to Gabe.

"On the charge of murder, what is your verdict?"

"Guilty, Your Honor."

TWENTY-NINE

IN THE MOMENT OF SILENCE THAT FOLLOWED, GABE Conroy's gaze turned from Judge Mintz to Matthew Bissonet, standing beside Andrew at the defense table. Then the courtroom erupted in cries of astonishment and surprise, which Mintz tried unsuccessfully to gavel into silence. Andrew immediately gripped Matthew's arm and made him sit down.

"We will appeal."

"Andrew, I didn't do it."

"I know you didn't. And Quarles certainly did not prove you did. The conviction will be overturned."

The confidence he felt was, alas, the same he had felt before the trial began. The verdict had not altered the fact that Matthew was innocent. Nor did he think any objective review of the transcript would conclude that he had lost and Quarles had won the case. In the meantime, however, they had to rise and hear Mintz announce a date for sentencing. Matthew's expression was heartrending. He had hoped he had seen the last of that jail cell.

"This is just a setback, Matthew. I won't rest until you're free."

Susannah and Gerald did not accompany him when he went with Matthew and the guards to the holding room. Matthew's spirits had lifted with Andrew's assurance that eventually he would be freed, and the verdict overturned.

"I never thought an innocent person could be convicted in an American courtroom."

"Convictions are subject to appeal."

"Thank God you're my lawyer."

And thank God for small favors. Matthew would not have been the first defendant to blame his lawyer for a guilty verdict. Returning to his office, Andrew tried to blame himself. What had he overlooked that might have swung the balance? The one thing he would do differently was to not accept Gabe Conroy as a member of the jury.

He was met by silence when he arrived at his office. He lifted his brows as if in surprise.

"What's this? We've got work to do. There is an appeal to be filed and I want it done as soon as possible. I am not going to abandon Matthew now."

"I can't believe the verdict," Susannah said.

"They must have forgotten your summary, Andrew," Gerald said. "It was masterful."

"Not masterful enough. Let's make up for it in the appeal."

Late that afternoon, Emily Nichols came in to tell him that Jane Bissonet wished to talk with him.

"What line is she on?"

"She asked you to come to her house."

It was a visit Andrew would have liked to avoid, but of course he could not. Jane had not been in court and sooner or later he would have to speak to the mother of the convicted man.

Work had driven from his mind the sour memory of defeat, and he had seen what a tonic his confidence had been for Susannah and Gerald. But speaking with Edgar's widow he would feel again the unaccustomed sense of failure, to which would be added the realization that he had let the Bissonet and Spencer families down. Again, he remembered the bright victorious gaze of Gabe Conroy.

"Would you like me to come along, Andrew?" Susannah asked, realizing how he felt.

"Better not."

She had seen him lose in court. There was no need for her to witness the muted disappointment of Jane Bissonet.

They talked in the large room at the back of the house that was on the level of the course. Out there in the carefully planned layout of grass and rough, sand and green, was the blueprint of peace and vacation from care. But now Andrew saw it as an ironic contrast to this anguished confrontation with Matthew's mother.

"I lost the case, Mrs. Bissonet."

"I did not believe it when I heard."

"I am already at work on an appeal. I cannot believe that a higher court will not throw out this verdict. The prosecution did not prove its case. There is reasonable doubt."

"Matthew did not kill his father."

"I don't believe for a moment that he did. Nor do I think that Cecil Quarles established that he did."

"You cannot prove what did not happen."

"No."

There was no point in telling Jane the vast difference between what is known in the real world and what is admitted into the carefully circumscribed world of the court. The jury system is an unequivocal blessing, one of the bastions of justice, but it is not infallible. The appeals court exists to make up for the possible deficiencies of a jury. Jane said something so low, he did not understand.

"I'm sorry."

"I said I did it." Her voice strengthened. "I took Edgar's life. Matthew's arrest was a nuisance and an inconvenience but I counted on his being acquitted. Now I must speak up."

Andrew smiled sadly. "Don't, Jane. I understand how you must feel. But that isn't going to help Matthew."

"Andrew, I did it. I came up behind him and pulled the bag over his head and left him sitting there, struggling to breathe and then lurching when his heart betrayed him." She looked to where the cart must have been. "I don't think he even knew who had done it. He had betrayed me but I did not want him to know that finally, after all these years, I was taking my revenge."

"For what?"

"For his infidelity." She sighed and looked up at the leaves of a cottonwood, rolling lazily in the slight wind. "Perhaps many men stray once or twice and then it is over. In Edgar's case, I am sure there was only this one affair. It very nearly ended our marriage, which would have been a great scandal in Wyler. But the woman went away and years passed and our marriage achieved another level of peace. Until his daughter arrived, first to work in the office, then to be brought into our home!"

It was becoming difficult to hear this as simply a mother's effort to save her son. Jane spoke in such deliberate tones, from time to time pointing to show where Edgar had sat on the patio and how she had approached him.

"You stopped for a plastic bag?"

"There was no need to. Edgar always took one with him onto the course, for Kleenex, cigar wrappers. He was very conscientious about litter."

"Where was the plastic bag?"

"On the seat beside him. I picked it up and slipped it over his head, bringing it tightly down, from behind so he could not see me."

"And then left him there?"

Jane looked at him. "I couldn't stay there while he . . ." Another sigh. "While he died. I went inside, just for a few minutes, and when I came out to remove the plastic bag, Edgar was gone. Andrew, my heart leaped. I began to think I hadn't really done it, that it was a hallucination. Had he driven onto the course and it was there his heart failed him? When there was no report of a plastic bag I was sure of it."

Andrew felt the eyes of Gabe Conroy on him. Why hadn't he or Quarles or anyone else suspected Jane? She was in the house all along, she had motive and opportunity, and now she was confessing her guilt. Would any other woman have been so invisible to the eyes of suspicion as the aristocratic Mrs. Bissonet? Her story was plausible, flawless, and Andrew did not believe it.

"What do you intend to do, Jane?"

"Are you asking as my lawyer?"

"All right."

"Then tell me what to do."

He could tell her he disbelieved her story, but he didn't. Even if her story were true, the important thing was to prevent her from telling it to anyone else.

"For the moment, Jane, this will be a confidence between you and me. Let the appeal go through. If the conviction is overturned, you will be in exactly the same position you would have been if Matthew had been found innocent. If the appeal is not successful, we can talk again."

"But I could get Matthew released from jail now."

"Perhaps. Perhaps not. I think he would rather be in jail for a little more time than have his mother take his place."

She wanted to know more about the appeal, and he told her, sensing this was the most productive line of discussion. When she called him, she had already imagined herself in the role of defendant, and she did not easily give way to his suggestion that, for the moment at least, she must tell no one else what she had told him.

"You would help a murderer escape justice?"

"One case at a time, Jane. First let me get Matthew's conviction overturned."

When he left he had secured her agreement, but any satisfaction he felt was dimmed by the memory of the expression on Gabe Conroy's face. The foreman of the jury may have been influenced by his past differences with Edgar to take revenge on his son, while all the time being unconscious of his motivation. But was not he himself influenced by favorable prejudice in not taking Jane seriously? How vivid her account had been, how plausible her explanation of what had happened. Nothing that anyone else had testified to, nothing that Andrew knew, conflicted with her story. If Matthew was innocent, as Andrew was convinced he was, someone had to be guilty. And who else had the motive and opportunity Jane had had?

He found that he could not tell Susannah what Jane had told him. Nor was this due to professional scruples. He always told Susannah everything without any fear that he was breaking a confidence. She would die before revealing what he told her and, since she seemed half his own soul, telling her was like talking to himself. But on this occasion he could not repeat to her what he had heard.

191

"I explained to her about the appeal," he said.

"How is she taking the verdict?"

"She would like to take Matthew's place."

That is as close as he came to telling her.

The following day, he left Gerald laboring over the appeal and drove to the golf course alone. Patty Cermac, dressed in a manner midway between her work clothes and the outfit she had worn in court, was already on the putting green. When he signed Patty in as his guest, Jack Wirth came out of the back room with a surprised expression.

"What did she tell you her handicap is, Andrew?"

"Does she have one?"

"A three."

"I'd put her down as a scratch golfer."

"Just so you know. I don't want you getting sand-bagged by the help."

"Why don't you join us, Jack?"

"I wish I could." Jack rubbed his chin. "Why don't you play the back nine? That way you can avoid the sprinklers."

"We'll play through them."

"I wish you wouldn't."

Jack's concern was odd. Since when did he think sprinklers would deter Andrew Broom from golfing?

Patty said, "That was this morning, Mr. Wirth. Joe had them turned off at eleven."

If this relieved Jack, he gave no sign of it. Andrew was intent on playing the holes that had figured in the trial he had just lost.

Patty's drive had a little tail on it and she ended in the left rough, necessitating an iron shot that could not reach the green, but she was on in three, close to the hole, and got her par, tying Andrew. If he had thought he would be giving her advice on this round, he was mistaken. Any tips he had would be given later, when he was sure the match was his. He was only one up when they reached the fifth tee. After their drives, hers looking like a clone of his, Andrew settled behind the wheel of the cart.

"This is the hole from which you did not see Edgar driven onto the seventh fairway."

She took off her cap and settled it back on her head. "If you hadn't found out I was lying, Mr. Wirth would have."

"Oh?"

"I told you he passed me as I was mowing, coming from home on his usual morning route. Sooner or later, it would have occurred to him that I hadn't been able to see seven from five. Not that it really matters now, right?"

"Right?"

"I mean, I shouldn't have moved the old man, but it didn't change anything, did it?"

He told her it didn't, but as they moved down the fairway to their balls, his thoughts multiplied and assumed new linkups. He turned to Patty.

"What time would it have been when you saw Jack that morning?"

"Oh, not that again."

"Was it when you first started mowing this fairway, or had you been doing it for a while?"

"I was just trying to forget that I'm usually on a mower when I travel over these fairways. I guess I was half done when I saw him. You should ask him. He's like clockwork."

Andrew did not pursue it, but when he hit his second

193

shot he was thinking of what Claire had told him of their blighted friendship with Mona and Jack Wirth. Jack's jealousy had driven them apart. Jack's suspicion of Matthew Bissonet. Andrew popped his shot and it ended well short of the green. Patty's ball dropped softly in front of the hole and rolled to within millimeters of the stick. They were even when they holed out.

It was when they were playing seven that he made up his mind what he would do.

"Would you mind if we stop after nine holes, Patty?"

"What's wrong?"

"Nothing. I just thought of something I have to do."

"All right."

"Patty, I'm sorry. We'll golf again. I promise. And I'll tell you now I think you have an excellent game. Have you ever entered a tournament?"

"A tournament? I work for a living."

"I'm going to sponsor you. You don't belong on a lawn mower."

This prospect placated her and they parted at the ninth hole. "Why don't you go ahead and play the back nine?"

He watched her head down the tenth fairway after her drive and then took another cart and headed across the course toward the seventh fairway.

He passed Edgar's house and then went diagonally across the fairway toward Jack Wirth's house. He was hoping that Mona would be there, wanting to talk to her first. If she wasn't, he would head back to the pro shop and talk with Jack. When he came across the Wirth lawn, Mona, who had been sunning herself, sat up. Her outfit provided maximum exposure to the sun, which seemed reasonable enough if you were sunning

194

yourself, but Andrew was struck as he had never been before by Mona's beauty. Her welcoming off-center smile as she recognized him reminded Andrew slightly of the perfidious Dorothy and he wondered if Jack's suspicions were unfounded. Mona was undeniably a flirt.

"I'm drinking iced tea but if you want something stronger just go inside and help yourself."

"I'd like a glass of ice water."

"Is the supply in your veins low?"

He stepped through the French doors and went on to the kitchen. Mona followed him. Inside, her costume seemed skimpier than it had outside. Andrew decided he should get right to the point.

"Matthew Bissonet has been found guilty of his father's murder."

"I was so sorry to hear that." Her regret was obviously sincere.

"I feel I let him down."

"Oh, I don't believe that."

"He is innocent, Mona."

"Of course he is."

"You're that sure?"

"Jack and I are good friends of Matthew and his wife."

"Still?"

This surprised her, but then she changed expression. "I suppose he would have told his lawyer everything."

"Jack was jealous of Matthew?"

"Jack would have been jealous of Edgar if it had occurred to him."

Andrew laughed, relieved to have gotten to the heart of the matter so easily.

"People on the grounds crew tell me they could set

195

their watches by Jack. What time does he leave for work in the morning."

"Before I'm up, I'll tell you that. He makes a light breakfast and then he's off."

"He drives to the clubhouse?"

"Not by car. He goes back and forth by electric cart." She made a face. "Such a silent, sneaky contraption."

"What time does he leave?"

"Would you believe six o'clock?" She rolled her eyes incredulously.

"Where's the ice?"

"Here, I'll do it."

She took the glass, put it under the ice machine on the refrigerator door, and pushed. Cubes cascaded into the glass. She filled the glass at the tap, then turned to him, holding it in both hands, not moving.

"Here."

Andrew hesitated, then crossed to her, reaching for the glass, but she turned, laughing, keeping it away from him. Andrew tried to take hold of the glass, a mistake, because Mona began to squirm against him, laughing in an abandoned way.

"What the hell are you doing with my wife!"

Andrew turned to see an irate Jack Wirth advancing on him. His face was twisted in rage.

"I wondered why you didn't finish your round. Patty too tame for you, or what?"

"Jack, take it easy."

But Jack lunged at him, hands outstretched, a mindless enraged movement. Andrew grabbed his wrists, and turned, causing Jack to lose his balance and crash against the kitchen table. A banshee wail went up from Mona. Jack kicked out and caught Andrew's shin. Mona scooted past and ran out of the room. Jack roared an obscenity after her, regained his balance, and swung at Andrew. Enough was enough. Andrew drove a fist into Jack's midsection and, when the pro doubled over, he brought his other fist sharply upward, catching his chin. Jack's eyes glazed over and he slumped to the floor. Andrew stopped, picked him up, and carried him out to the patio where a wild-eyed Mona stood, still holding the glass of ice water.

"What happened to him?"

Andrew dumped Jack into a lawn chair, took the water from Mona, and dashed it into her husband's face. Jack sputtered and tried to sit up but Andrew pushed him back. He drew up a chair.

"All right, Jack. You're going to tell me what you did to Edgar Bissonet."

"What the hell are you talking about?" He looked past Andrew at Mona. "Get out of here, you bitch. Pack your things and go."

Andrew gripped Jack's wet shirt front and shook him. "Forget about her, Jack."

Jack looked pleadingly at Andrew and tears welled in his eyes. A sob escaped him. "You don't know what it's like. I don't blame you, Andrew. I know her too well. But don't be flattered. She goes for anything that moves."

"Matthew Bissonet?"

"Him I blame. We were friends. I trusted him."

Andrew didn't like the implication of the remark, but this was no time to take umbrage.

"He didn't kill his father, Jack."

"Tell it to the jury."

"I see things now I didn't see when I talked to the jury, Jack. Now I know what you did that morning. I have found a witness."

A sneer refused to form on his face. He was thinking. "Patty!"

"Tell me about it, Jack."

"What did she say?"

"I'd rather hear it from you, Jack."

"I want a drink."

"Afterward."

"First I want to know what Patty said she saw."

"Jack, you know what she saw. You and I know why you did it. You did it to get revenge on Matthew, didn't you? You saw him coming back from his father's house, you saw the old man sitting there on his patio. He wouldn't be alarmed if you stopped by on your way to the clubhouse. All you had to do was pick up the plastic bag off his seat and pull it over his head. And Matthew would get the blame."

"She saw all that?"

Andrew managed not to show his elation. My God, of course it had been Jack. Now he felt he should have known this all along. Mona, a step or two inside the French doors, had obviously heard what had been said. Now she came out onto the patio.

"You killed that sweet old man?"

Her question brought Jack out of the chair in a single motion and he went after Mona, whose wail followed her into the house. Only by tackling Jack could Andrew stop him. This time he rolled him onto his stomach and pulled his arm sharply up behind him. A grunt of pain and then, after a moment, weeping. A full minute went by before Mona appeared in the open doors.

"Call Sheriff Cleary."

THIRTY

AT THE *DEALER,* REBECCA PRELL EXPLAINED TO Foster that the whole thing followed a pattern—an older man infatuated with a young woman is liable to do anything.

"Jack Wirth?"

"His wife is younger than he is."

"Two or three years at least."

Rebecca became prettily pensive and Foster frowned away his reaction to the young reporter.

"Of course it works both ways," she said.

"How so?"

"I'll bet Mona Wirth flirted with Edgar too."

"Like Elena?"

"Yes!"

"But she's his daughter."

Rebecca searched for some reply, then gave it up.

"I'm beginning to wonder if there's an older man in your life," Foster said.

Her smile unnerved him. She acted as if he had discovered her secret. Foster was filled with a panic that only left him when Bruce Hutton came to pick Rebecca up.

"How old are you, Bruce?" Foster asked.

"Twenty-seven. Why?"

"That's a good age."

Good enough to make him an older man for Rebecca. Watching them leave, Foster felt a faint regret. Ah well, maybe he was meant for an older woman.

A week before the reversal of Matthew Bissonet's guilty verdict in the death of his father came down from the appeals court, Jane followed her husband in death.

"It is sad that she did not live long enough to learn of his official vindication," Susannah said.

"Yes."

"It is sadder still to think that the trial and its outcome hastened her death."

It was a moment for philosophical remarks, even those for which Andrew knew there was no foundation. He had dismissed Jane's fanciful tale as he had earlier dismissed the speculation of Claire Bissonet about Jack Wirth's jealousy. In the court of his conscience, he got a going over for the way he had handled the death of Edgar Bissonet.

"Your record is unblemished," Gerald said proudly.

"I should have won an acquittal in the first place."

"Don't be so hard on yourself."

"If Jack Wirth hadn't confessed, it's possible the appeals court would have turned me down."

"Impossible."

"I thought conviction was impossible."

It was churlish to resent a satisfactory resolution of the murder of Edgar Bissonet. But Andrew was weary of the lot of them. He told Matthew that Gerald would represent him in his efforts to have Edgar's will thrown out. Elena Maria would get no more than the legitimate children from Edgar's estate.

"I am after the brokerage account he kept for her, Andrew. He made her wealthy."

"Let it go, Matthew. Let it go."

"If it weren't for my children, I might."

How like his father he was. It was Edgar's paternal feeling for the daughter of his adulterous love of long ago that had divided his family. One thing Jane had not feigned was her resentment of Edgar's loyalty to his illegitimate daughter. In the event, Elena waived all claim to an inheritance from her father.

"That is very good of you," Andrew said.

"No. It is wise. Hector would disown me if I took a cent of Edgar's money." She smiled sweetly. "My investments are another matter."

"Are you going back to Chile?"

"There is nothing to keep me here. My half-brothers and -sisters will have nothing to do with me."

"I would like to meet your mother some time."

"She is a very beautiful woman."

"She would have to be," Andrew said gallantly.

And it was gallantry that stopped him from telling Elena about the poems Edgar had sent to her mother in Santiago over the years. They were plagiarized, every one of them. Poems in which the name of the true dedicatee had been replaced by Elena or Elena Maria, as scansion required. It seemed somehow fitting that Edgar should have expressed his imaginary sentiments in counterfeit coin. Yet in a way he had played fair. It was daring enough to steal Shakespeare's seventy-sixth sonnet, but its sestet could be taken as a confession of sorts.

O, know, Elena, I always write of you,
And you and love are still my argument;
So all my best is dressing old words new,
Spending again what is already spent:
For as the sun is daily new and old,
So is my love, still telling what is told.

Dear Reader:

I hope you enjoyed reading this Large Print mystery. If you are interested in reading other Beeler Large Print Mystery titles or any other Beeler Large Print titles, ask your librarian or write to me at

Thomas T. Beeler, *Publisher*
Post Office Box 659
Hampton Falls, New Hampshire 03844

You can also call me at 1-800-818-7574 and I will send you my latest catalogue.

Audrey Lesko chooses the titles I publish in Large Print. Our aim is to provide good books by outstanding authors—books we both enjoyed reading and liked well enough to want to share. We warmly welcome any suggestions for new titles and authors.

Sincerely,